THE ADVENTURES OF FELUDA
THE HOUSE OF DEATH

Satyajit Ray (1921-1992) was one of the greatest filmmakers of his time, renowned for films like *Pather Panchali, Charulata, Aranyer Din Ratri* and *Ghare Baire*. He was awarded the Oscar for Lifetime Achievement by the Academy of Motion Picture Arts and Science in 1992, and in the same year, was also honoured with the Bharat Ratna.

Ray was also a writer of repute, and his short stories, novellas, poems and articles, written in Bengali, have been immensely popular ever since they first began to appear in the children's magazine *Sandesh* in 1961. Among his most famous creations are the master sleuth Feluda and the scientist Professor Shonku.

*

Gopa Majumdar has translated several works from Bengali to English, the most notable of these being Ashapurna Debi's *Subarnalata*, Taslima Nasrin's *My Girlhood*, and Bibhutibhushan Bandyopadhyay's *Aparajito*, for which she won the Sahitya Akademi Award in 2002. She has translated several volumes of Satyajit Ray's short stories and all of the Feluda stories for Penguin Books India. She is currently translating Ray's Professor Shonku stories, which are forthcoming in Puffin.

Read the other Adventures of Feluda in Puffin

THE ADVENTURES OF FELUDA

THE HOUSE OF DEATH

Satyajit Ray

Translated from the Bengali by Gopa Majumdar

PUFFIN BOOKS

PUFFIN BOOKS

Penguin Books India (P) Ltd., 11 Community Centre, Panchsheel Park, New Delhi
110 017, India

Penguin Books Ltd., 80 Strand, London WC2R 0RL, UK

Penguin Putnam Inc., 375 Hudson Street, New York, NY 10014, USA

Penguin Books Australia Ltd., 250 Camberwell Road, Camberwell, Victoria 3124, Australia

Penguin Books Canada Ltd., 10 Alcorn Avenue, Suite 300, Toronto, Ontario M4V
3B2, Canada

Penguin Books (NZ) Ltd., Cnr Rosedale and Airborne Roads, Albany, Auckland,
New Zealand

Penguin Books (South Africa) (Pty) Ltd, 24 Sturdee Avenue, Rosebank 2196, South
Africa

First published in Puffin by Penguin Books India 2003
Copyright © The Estate of Satyajit Ray 2003
This translation copyright © Penguin Books India 2003

Typeset in Garamond by Mantra Virtual Services, New Delhi
Printed at Thomson Press, Noida

This is a work of fiction. Names, characters, places and incidents are either the
product of the author's imagination or are used fictitiously, and any resemblance to
any actual person, living or dead, events, or locales is entirely coincidental.

DUNGRU'S STORY

Dungru laid his instrument on the grass that was still wet with the morning dew, and began singing. He had a pretty good voice. The song he was now singing was one he had heard only once before. Yet, he had picked it up, almost without making an effort. It was a song a beggar usually sang just outside Hanuman Phatak. But he played an instrument, too. Shyam Gurung, the local greengrocer, had an instrument like that. Dungru had borrowed it for the day, but had already realized playing it wasn't half as easy as singing. Who knew running a bow over a few strings could be so difficult?

Dungru's voice rose. There was a maize field in front of him, in which a couple of buffaloes and three goats were roaming freely. There was no one else in sight. Behind him was a very steep hill. Just under it, not far from the mound on which he sat, stood an almond tree. The little house in the distance with a tiled roof was where he lived. His father owned this maize field. There were other hills and several mountain peaks dimly visible through the morning mist. One of these, called 'Machhipuchh' because it was shaped like a fishtail, had started to turn pink.

Dungru began the second line of the song, but had to break off abruptly. A strange rumble in the hill behind him made him spring to his feet and jump to one side. In the next instant, a large boulder rolled down the hill and went past him, crushing his instrument and missing him by inches.

Dungru could hardly believe his luck. But before his heartbeat could get back to normal, something else happened: something much more unexpected and far worse than a rolling boulder. But, like the boulder, it came crashing down the hill, struck against the almond tree and fell to the ground, together with several broken branches. What on earth was that? He gaped, his mouth hanging open. Good heavens, it was a man! Not just any man, but a well-dressed babu, probably from a big city. There was blood on his head, his face, and chin. One of his legs was folded under him at a very odd angle. Was he dead? No. Dungru saw him move his head.

Then he remembered the others. There was a group of men camping out near the spring across the main road. Dungru had often stared in amazement at the colour of their hair and their beards. No one that he knew in his own village had hair like that. And certainly no one had a beard. But if anyone could help this man, it had to be those men. They knew Dungru. They had bought maize from him and given him money almost every day.

Dungru began running.

'Hi, Joe, come here quickly!' shouted one of them on seeing Dungru.

'Why, what's up?'

Dungru stood panting. He couldn't speak their language. In fact, he was too breathless to speak at all. So he just rolled his eyes and stuck his tongue out. Then he pointed at the hill. The man caught on immediately.

'OK. Jeep. Go . . . Jeep!'

Their jeep had all the colours of a rainbow. Dungru had never seen a vehicle like that. He jumped into it. Joe, Mark, Dennis, and Bruce joined him.

'Jesus Christ!' one of them exclaimed softly when Dungru took them to the exact spot where the injured man still lay on the ground. All of them bent over him. Mark, who had left studying medicine in Minnesota, checked his pulse. Then they picked him up and placed him carefully in the jeep.

The nearest hospital was in Kathmandu, thirty-three kilometres from here.

CHAPTER 1

There was something special about Feluda's palm. The line called 'headline' that's supposed to indicate one's intelligence, was exceptionally long and clear. Feluda did not believe in palmistry, but had read up on the subject. Lalmohan Babu, who believed in it wholeheartedly, had once asked Feluda to show him his palm. Feluda had obliged with a grin, but Lalmohan Babu had failed to share his amusement. He had inspected the headline, then said, 'Amazing, amazing!' After this, he had opened his own palm, looked at it and sighed deeply. I had had to try very hard not to laugh.

One of my uncles could read palms. I had heard him make reasonably accurate statements about one's past and make predictions for the future that often turned out to be true. Some people, I was told, could look at a person's face and tell him about his future. But I didn't know it was possible to place one's little finger in the middle of a person's forehead and reveal what the future had in store for him. I saw this being done only when we visited Puri.

Incessant power shedding and a temperature of 110°F had driven us out of Calcutta. The power crisis had got so bad that Lalmohan Babu's latest novel could not be printed in April. He was most annoyed at this, particularly as it was his first crime thriller with a touch of the supernatural. As a matter of fact, it was Feluda who had given him the idea. 'Ghosts and spooks go very well with flickering candlelight.' Lalmohan Babu had taken this seriously and written *Frankenstein in Frankfurt*. When he learnt it could not be published as scheduled, he came straight to our house and said, 'We cannot go on living in this city. Besides, you've heard of the skylab, haven't you?'

There was really no reason to assume the skylab would come crashing down on Calcutta, but Lalmohan Babu kept saying that a large portion of it might, since the entire city of Calcutta appeared to have caught the 'evil eye'.

Feluda is normally extremely adaptable. I have seen him remain perfectly unperturbed even under the most trying circumstances. If he had to spend a whole night at a railway station and the waiting room happened to be full, he'd quite happily stretch out on the platform. But there was one thing he couldn't do without: reading in bed for a few hours before going to sleep. Weeks and weeks of power cuts had deprived him of this one luxury he allowed himself to indulge in. This had made him rather cross. He had tried practising card tricks, written limericks, and tried many other things to amuse himself. Long periods of darkness, I had hoped, would result in more crime. But sadly, no interesting cases had come his way. He was, in short, utterly bored.

This was perhaps the reason why he appeared to agree with Lalmohan Babu and said, 'Really, the City of Joy has been causing us a lot of grief, hasn't it? I can put up with the physical discomfort, but constant disturbances at work, having to give up reading at night, not even being able to think because of mosquitoes . . . these are very difficult to live with.'

'Orissa, I hear, has got excess power,' Lalmohan Babu observed.

This led to a discussion about Orissa, Puri, the sea beach in Puri and the hotel called Neelachal that had recently opened there, and was owned by Lalmohan Babu's landlord's classmate.

Unfortunately, it turned out that we couldn't get reservations before mid-June. 'Never mind, we'll go in June,' said Feluda. Eventually, we left on 21 June by the Puri Express. It was decided that Lalmohan Babu's driver would take his car and get to Puri by road a day later. We might have gone by car ourselves, but Lalmohan Babu had a sudden attack of nerves at the last minute and said, 'Suppose there's a storm or something on the way? Suppose we get stranded?'

But he agreed having our own car was a good idea, since we intended visiting a few other places. Hence the two different travel arrangements.

Our journey was uneventful, except for the fourth passenger in our four-berth compartment. He was the only exciting thing that happened. First we saw him fit a cigarette into a holder that seemed to be made of gold. Then he took out a gold-plated lighter ('At least three thousand rupees,' Feluda whispered) to light it. His cigarette case was also golden, as were his cuff links, the frames of his glasses and the three rings he wore. While climbing down from the upper berth, one of his feet accidentally brushed against Lalmohan Babu's shoulder. He gave an embarrassed smile at this and said, 'Sorry.' One of his teeth, we all noted, flashed as he opened his mouth. When he got off at Puri with us and disappeared with a coolie and his luggage, Lalmohan Babu sighed.

'We didn't even get to know the man's name. Have you ever seen so much gold on a man, Tapesh?' he asked.

'There was a very easy way to find out his name, Lalmohan Babu,' Feluda replied. 'Didn't you see the reservation list at Howrah? That man is called M.L. Hingorani.'

Chapter 2

'This is a six-star hotel,' Lalmohan Babu declared, nodding with approval after checking in at Neelachal.

'No hotel can claim to be five-star unless it has a swimming pool; and five-star is the maximum rating a hotel can get. Can you spot a swimming pool anywhere, Lalmohan Babu? Or are you counting the sea as this hotel's very own, private pool? If so, your rating is fully justified.'

We went in to have lunch, after which Lalmohan Babu continued the argument with fresh vigour. 'What lovely food, Felu Babu! Their cook is absolutely brilliant. I had no idea koftas made of green banana could be so delicious. Besides, see how clean everything is, such beautiful carpets and furnishings, and a totally uninterrupted power supply, not to mention the sea breeze . . . why shouldn't I call it a six-star hotel?'

Feluda laughed in agreement. What might happen to the hotel in a few years was impossible to tell, but right now it was certainly in very good condition. Feluda and I were sharing a double room. Lalmohan Babu had the next room, which he was sharing with a businessman from Calcutta. We had briefly met Shyamlal Barik, the manager. He had promised to come and have a chat with us in the evening.

The hotel was really very close to the sea. The sandy beach was only a minute's walk from the main gate. The last time I visited Puri, I was only five years old. Feluda had come here many times, but, to our surprise, we learnt that this was Lalmohan Babu's first visit.

'What's there to be so surprised about?' he asked, a little annoyed. 'There are so many things in Calcutta I haven't yet seen. Would you believe it, there's that famous Jain temple only three miles from my house, but I have never been there!' Now, standing before the sea, he suddenly remembered a poem written by his favourite poet, Baikuntha Mallik. 'When I was twelve,' he told me, 'I recited this poem in a competition and won a prize. Listen to it carefully, Tapesh, and note how beautiful even modern free verse can be:

In these roaring waves,
I hear the call of infinity;
when on these sandy beaches,
stand I, so eagerly,
on one leg.'

'One leg? Why one leg?' Feluda sounded puzzled. 'Was the poet identifying himself with a crane? That must be it, for it would be quite difficult for a man to stand on one leg on the sand, hour after hour, in this strong wind. But never mind your poet. Look at the sand over there. See those prints? Do you think that might have any significance?'

The footprints had come from the east, and made their way to the western side. A smaller mark by the side of these indicated a stick. Lalmohan Babu stared at these for a few seconds and said, 'Well, shoes and perhaps a walking stick . . . that much is clear, but what special significance could it have?'

'Topshe, what do you think?'

'Usually, people hold a stick in their right hand. These marks are on the left.'

Feluda thumped my shoulder. 'Good! The man is probably left-handed.'

There weren't many people about. Three small *nulia* children were busy collecting crabs and seashells. There were other hotels a little way ahead, where no doubt we'd find many more visitors. Just as we began walking in that direction, someone called, 'Mr Ganguli!'

We turned to find it was Mr Srinivas Som, Lalmohan Babu's plump and cheerful roommate. We had already met him. He owned a saree shop in Calcutta.

'Aren't you coming?' he asked Lalmohan Babu. 'He said to be there by six o'clock sharp.'

Lalmohan Babu gave Feluda a sidelong glance. 'I didn't tell you, Felu Babu,' he said hesitantly, 'because I thought you might not be interested.'

'Didn't tell me what?'

'Er . . . Mr Som told me about a man who lives here. He has an extraordinary power. He can place a finger on the forehead and talk about one's future.'

'Whose forehead?'

'The person who goes to him, naturally.'

'You mean he can actually read what's written in one's destiny?'

'Yes, supposedly.'

'Very well. I have no wish to have my future read, but let's all go and see where he lives.'

Mr Som led the way. We followed him, walking towards the east, past a colony of *nulias* and groups of visitors, and up a sandy slope. Then we saw an abandoned house, partially submerged in the sand. Mr Som walked past it, but stopped before another house only a few yards away. This house had three storeys and was obviously in a far better condition. The astrologer, it turned out, occupied two rooms on the ground floor. There was a big gate. On one side was written, 'Sagarika'. A marble slab on the other side said, 'D.G. Sen'. It was an old-fashioned house, but whoever had had it built had good taste. There was a garden, a portion of which was visible from the gate.

'The owner lives on the second floor,' said Mr Som. 'Ah, here we are . . . this is Laxman Bhattacharya's room.'

There were nearly a dozen people waiting outside on the veranda. No doubt they were all Mr Bhattacharya's clients. Lalmohan Babu said, 'Jai Guru!' and walked in with Mr Som. We came away.

'What did your forehead reveal?' asked Feluda about an hour later, as Lalmohan Babu swept into our room in great excitement.

'Incredible, extraordinary, absolutely uncanny!' Lalmohan Babu replied. 'He told me everything about my past—whooping cough at the age of seven, an accident when I was eighteen, which left me with a dislocated kneecap, then the publication of my first novel, my spectacular popularity, and he even told me how many editions my next book will have.'

'And the skylab? Did he tell you whether or not it's going to fall on your head?'

'You can joke all you like, Felu Babu, but I think you ought to visit him. In fact, I insist that you do. He seemed to know about you. He said I was very lucky to have a good friend, and even gave your description!'

'What about my profession? Did he say anything about that?'

'He said my friend was very hard-working, and intelligent, with a great interest in many subjects, and had remarkable powers of observation. Is that close enough for you?'

'May I come in?' said a voice at the door.

We turned to find the manager, Shyamlal Barik, waiting to come in with a small box of paan in his hand. Feluda invited him in, and he opened his box at once. Our room was filled with the sweet smell of paan-masala. 'Have one,' he offered. Then, looking at our faces, he laughed. 'Don't worry, there's no tobacco in any of these,' he assured us. We helped ourselves. Feluda lit a Charminar.

'Tell me, Mr Barik, what is D.G. Sen's full name?' he asked.

'I've only just been to his house, and it never occurred to me to ask!' exclaimed Lalmohan Babu.

Shyamlal Barik smiled. 'The truth is, Mr Mitter, that I don't know his full name. I doubt if anyone does. Everyone calls him D.G. Sen. Some even call him DG Babu.'

'Doesn't he go out much?'

'He used to. Last year, he went to Bhutan or Sikkim or some such place. He returned about six months ago. We've hardly ever seen him since he came back.'

'Do you know why he suddenly turned into a recluse?'

Shyamlal Barik shook his head. 'Did he build that house?' Feluda went on.

'No. It was built by his father. You may have heard of him. Do you know about Sen Perfumers?'

'Yes, yes. But they've gone out of business, haven't they? S.N. Sen's Sensational Essences. Is that what you mean?'

'Yes. DG is S.N. Sen's son. Their business was doing very well. They had three houses in Calcutta, one here in Puri and one in Madhupur. But, sadly, no one took any interest in the business when S.N. Sen died. He had two sons. DG is the younger of the two, I think. S.N. Sen had left a will, dividing all his property between his sons. DG got this house. He may have had a job at one time—I don't think he ever bothered about the family business—but now he's retired and his sole interest is art.'

'Art?' Feluda suddenly seemed to recall something. 'Is he the one who has a collection of ancient manuscripts and scrolls?'

Uncle Sidhu had a few scrolls. Some of them were more than three hundred years old. Scrolls and manuscripts written before the advent of the printing press were called *puthi*. Feluda had once explained this to me. A long time ago, people used to write on the bark of a tree. Then they began to write on palm leaves and, finally, on paper. Uncle Sidhu had often lamented that people had forgotten these manuscripts which are an important part of our art and cultural heritage.

Shyamlal Barik nodded. 'Yes, those old manuscripts are his only passion in life. Many people come—even from abroad—to take a look at his collection.'

'Doesn't he have any children?'

'A son and daughter-in-law used to visit him occasionally, but I haven't seen them for ages. D.G. Sen himself came to live here only three years ago. He's a widower. He lives on the top floor. The ground floor has been rented out to an astrologer; and the rooms on the first floor are let out to tourists during the tourist season. At the moment, a retired judge and his wife are staying there.'

'I see.' Feluda stubbed out his cigarette.

'Would you like to meet him?' Mr Barik asked. 'He's a peculiar man, doesn't normally agree to meet outsiders. But if you have an interest in manuscripts . . .'

'I do,' Feluda interrupted him, 'but if I simply say I have an interest, that won't do, will it? I must do my homework before I meet someone who has a profound knowledge of old manuscripts.'

'That's no problem,' Mr Barik assured us. 'I'll take you to Satish Kanungo's house. It's just five minutes from here. He's a retired professor. There's probably no subject on earth he doesn't know about. You can have a chat with him, and do your homework.'

CHAPTER 3

The next morning, by the time I got up, Feluda had already called Professor Kanungo and gone over to his house. This surprised me, since I had no idea he was in such a hurry to meet the professor. My plans were different. I had wanted to spend the morning bathing in the sea. Feluda might have accompanied me. I asked Lalmohan Babu, but he said, 'Look Tapesh, at your age, I used to swim a lot. My butterfly-stroke often earned me applause from onlookers. But a small Calcutta swimming pool is not the same thing as the Bay of Bengal, surely you can see that? Besides, the sea in Puri is extremely treacherous. Had it been the sea in Bombay, I wouldn't have hesitated.'

He was right. It had rained the night before and was still cloudy and kind of oppressive. So we decided to wait until Feluda got back. 'Let's go and have a walk

on the beach,' Lalmohan Babu suggested. I agreed, and
we left soon after a breakfast of toast and eggs. Lalmohan
Babu seemed to be in a very good mood, possibly as a
result of what Laxman Bhattacharya had told him.

The beach was totally empty. A few boats were out
in the sea, but there was no sign of the nulia children.
A couple of crows were flying about, going near the
water as the waves receded, then flitting quickly away
as they came surging back again.

We walked on. A few minutes later, Lalmohan Babu
stopped suddenly. 'I have heard of people sunbathing
on a beach,' he observed, 'but do they also cloud-bathe?'
I could see what he meant. A man was lying on his
back about fifty yards away, at a spot where the beach
ended and a slope began. There was a bush on one
side. Had the man chosen to lie down a little to the left,
he would have been hidden from sight.

'Seems a bit odd, doesn't it?' Lalmohan Babu
whispered. I said nothing, but went forward to have
closer look. Why was the man lying here? It certainly
did not seem right.

Even from ten feet away, he looked as though he
was sleeping. But as we went a few steps further, we
realized with a shock that he was dead. His eyes were
open, and around his head was a pool of blood; or, at
least, it had been a pool hours ago, now it was a dark
patch on the sand.

The man had thick curly hair, thick eyebrows, a
heavy moustache and a clear complexion. He was
wearing a grey cotton jacket, white trousers and a blue
striped shirt. There were shoes on his feet, but no socks.

On one of his little fingers he wore a ring with a blue stone. His nails were long and dirty. The front pocket of his jacket was crammed with papers. I was sorely tempted to take them out and go through them quickly, just to find out who the man was. But Lalmohan Babu said, 'Don't touch anything.' There was actually no need to say this, for I knew from experience what one should or should not do in a case like this.

'We are the first to . . . to . . . discover, I think?' Lalmohan Babu asked, trying very hard to appear cool and nonchalant. But I could tell his mouth had gone dry. 'Yes, I think so, too,' I replied, feeling rather shaken myself. 'Well, we must report it.'

'Yes, yes, of course.'

We hurried back to the hotel to find that Feluda had returned.

'Judging by the fact that you forgot to wipe your feet before coming in and spread a few hundred grams of sand all over the floor, I assume you are greatly perturbed about something,' Feluda announced, looking at Lalmohan Babu. I spoke hastily before Lalmohan Babu could get the chance to exaggerate what we had seen. Feluda heard me in silence, then rang the police to explain in a few succinct words what had happened. Then he turned to me and asked just one question: 'Did you see a weapon anywhere near the body? A pistol or something?'

'No, Feluda.'

'But I'm absolutely certain the fellow isn't a Bengali,' Lalmohan Babu said firmly.

'Why do you say that?'

'Those eyebrows. They were joined. Bengalis don't have joined eyebrows. Nor do they have such a strong, firm jaw as this man. I shouldn't be surprised if he turns out to be from Bundelkhand.'

Feluda, in the meantime, had made an appointment with D.G. Sen. His secretary had asked him to call at 8.30 a.m. and not take more than fifteen minutes of Mr Sen's time. We left almost immediately.

On our way to Mr Sen's house, we noticed a small crowd near the dead body. It hadn't taken long for word to spread. This was no doubt a most unusual event. The police were already there. One of the officers spotted Feluda and stepped forward with a smile and an outstretched arm.

'Inspector Mahapatra!' Feluda exclaimed, shaking his hand warmly. 'We met over a case in Rourkela, didn't we?'

'Yes, I recognized you at once. Are you here on holiday?'

'Yes, that's the general idea. Who is the deceased?'

'No one from this area. His name is Rupchand Singh.'

'How did you find out?'

'There was a driving licence.'

'Where from?'

'Nepal.'

A gentleman wearing glasses made his way through the crowd, pushing the police photographer to one side. 'I saw the man yesterday. He was at a tea stall in Swargadwar Road. I was buying paan at the next stall. He asked me for a light, and then lit a cigarette.'

19

'How did he die?' Feluda asked Mr Mahapatra.

'Shot dead, I think. But we haven't yet found the weapon. This was tucked inside the driving licence. You may wish to take a look.' Feluda was handed a visiting card. Printed on one side was the name and address of a tailor's shop in Kathmandu. On the other side was written, in an unformed hand, the following words: A.K. Sarkar, 14 Meher Ali Road, Calcutta.

'Do let me know if you hear of anything interesting. We're staying at the Neelachal,' Feluda said.

We walked on, and soon arrived at D.G. Sen's house. Last evening, it had appeared impressive, even inviting. But now, under an overcast sky, it looked dark and forbidding.

A young man was standing outside the gate. He was probably a servant. On seeing us arrive, he came forward and said, 'Mitter Babu?'

'I am Mitter Babu,' Feluda replied.

'Please come with me.'

A cobbled path ran towards the garden. But, in order to get to the second floor, it was necessary to go to the rear of the house where there was a separate entrance. A few steps down the passage, Lalmohan Babu suddenly sprang back with a stifled exclamation. It turned out that his eyes had fallen on a long strip of paper. 'I th-thought it was a s-snake!' he exclaimed.

The servant left us at the bottom of the stairs. We saw another man coming down. 'Mr Mitter?' he asked with a smile, 'This way, please.' He looked about thirty-five, although his hairline had started to recede.

'I am Nishith Bose,' he said on the way up, 'I work

here as Durga Babu's secretary.'

'Durga Babu?'

'Durga Gati Sen. Everyone calls him D.G. Sen.'

There was a room on the right where the stairs ended. It was probably the secretary's, for I caught sight of a typewriter on a small table. On the left was a small corridor and two more rooms. Beyond this was a terrace. It was on the terrace that D.G. Sen was waiting for us.

A portion of the terrace was occupied by a greenhouse in which there were a few orchids. Mr Sen was sitting in a cane chair in the middle of the terrace. He appeared to be about sixty. Lalmohan Babu said afterwards, 'Personality with a capital P.' He was right. Mr Sen's complexion was very fair, his eyes were sharp, and he had a French beard. His broad shoulders indicated that once he must have been a regular visitor to a gym. But he didn't rise as we approached him. 'Namaskar,' he said from his chair. I found this odd, but the reason became clear as my eyes fell on his feet. His left foot was peeping out of his blue trousers. The whole foot was covered by a bandage.

Three chairs had been placed on the terrace. We took these and returned his greeting. 'We're very grateful to you,' Feluda told him, 'for allowing us to barge in like this. When I heard about your collection, I couldn't resist the temptation to come and see it.'

'I've had this interest for many years,' Mr Sen replied. His eyes held a faraway look. His voice was deep. It seemed to match his personality.

'My uncle—Siddheswar Bose—has a small collection of old manuscripts. I think you went to his house once, to look at what he had.'

'Yes, that's possible. I used to travel pretty widely in search of scrolls.'

'Is everything in your collection written in Bengali?'

'No, there are other languages. The best of the lot is in Sanskrit.'

'When was it written?'

'Twelfth century.'

This was followed by a short pause. There was no point in asking him to show us anything. He'd do so only if he felt like it.

'Lokenath!' Mr Sen called. Lokenath was probably the name of the servant, but why was he calling him?

Mr Bose appeared instead of Lokenath. Had he perhaps been standing behind the door? 'Lokenath's gone out, sir. Can I help?' he asked.

Mr Sen stretched out an arm. Mr Bose caught his hand and helped him get to his feet. 'Please follow me,' Mr Sen said to us. We trooped back to the corridor, and went into one of the two bedrooms. It was a large room, with a huge four-poster bed in it. Next to the bed was a Kashmiri table, on which stood a lamp, two medicine bottles and a glass. There was also a desk, a chair and lined against the wall, two Godrej safes.

'Open it,' Mr Sen commanded, looking at his secretary. Mr Bose fished out a bunch of keys from under a pillow and opened one of the safes.

I could see four shelves, each one of which was stacked with narrow, long packets, covered by red silk. A brief glance told me there were at least fifty of them. 'The other safe has a few more, but the really valuable—'

The really valuable one came out of a drawer in the first one. I noticed there was one more packet in the same drawer. Mr Bose untied the ribbon that held the piece of silk, revealing an eight-hundred-year-old scroll, held between two thin cylindrical pieces of wood.

'This one's called *Ashtadashasahasrika Pragya Paramita*,' said Mr Sen. 'There's one more, just as old, called *Kalpasutra*.'

The wooden cylinders were painted beautifully. Neither the colour of the paint, nor the intricate designs had dimmed with the passage of time. The manuscript itself had been written on a palm leaf. I could never have believed anyone's handwriting could be so beautiful.

'Where did you get this?' Feluda asked.

'Dharamshala.'

'Does that mean it came from Tibet, with the Dalai Lama?'

'Yes.'

Mr Sen took the scroll back from Feluda and passed it to Mr Bose. He tied it up again with the piece of silk and put it back in the safe.

'Were you sent here by your uncle?'

I was startled by the abruptness with which the question was asked. Feluda remained unruffled. 'No, sir,' he replied calmly.

'I am not a businessman, and I certainly don't wish to sell any of these. All I can do is show people what I've got, if anyone is interested.'

'My uncle could not afford to buy what you just showed me,' Feluda laughed. 'But then, I have no idea how much something like this might cost.'

'You couldn't possibly put a price on it. It's invaluable.'

'But there are people who'd quite happily pass these on to outsiders, aren't there? Aren't ancient manuscripts from India being sold to foreigners?'

'Yes, I am aware of that. Those who do this are criminals—confound them!'

'Doesn't your son share your interest?'

Mr Sen did not reply immediately. He seemed to grow a little preoccupied. Then he said, staring at the table, 'My son? I don't know him.'

'Sir, Mr Mitter's a famous detective, sir!' Mr Bose piped up, somewhat unnecessarily. D.G. Sen promptly brought his gaze back to focus it directly on Feluda. 'So what?' he barked, 'why should that make any difference? Have I killed anyone?'

Mr Barik had warned us about this. D.G. Sen really was a most peculiar man. But the next words he spoke made no sense at all.

'No detective could bring back what is lost. He who can do anything is still trying; closed doors are opening now, one by one. There's no need for a detective.'

None of us dared ask what he meant by this. In any case, our time was up. So we turned to go. 'I'll see you out,' Mr Bose said a little urgently. Feluda thanked Mr Sen once more, and we all said goodbye. Then we began climbing down the stairs.

'What's the matter with his foot?' Feluda asked Mr Bose.

'Gout,' he replied. 'He used to be very healthy and

fit, even a few months ago. But, over the last three months, he's been in a lot of pain and discomfort.'

'I noticed two bottles in his room. Were they for his gout?'

'Yes. One of them is to help him sleep. Laxman Babu gave it to him.'

'Who, the astrologer?' Lalmohan Babu asked in surprise.

'Yes, he knows many more things beside astrology, including ayurveda, as well as conventional medicine.'

'You don't say!'

'Oh yes. I've even heard him talk of old manuscripts when he's with Mr Sen.'

'What an extraordinary man!' Lalmohan Babu said admiringly.

Feluda remained silent.

CHAPTER 4

Lalmohan Babu wanted Feluda to meet Laxman Bhattacharya. But the astrologer was out and his room was locked. We came out of Sagarika and began walking back to our hotel. The beach was quite crowded by this time, for the clouds had dispersed and the sun had come out. There was a hotel on our right, not far from the beach. 'That's the Railway Hotel,' Feluda said. 'Most of these people are staying there.' We made our way through the crowd and moved away. Suddenly, someone called out: 'Mr Mitter!'

A tall gentleman was standing alone, away from groups of bathers, and smiling at Feluda. He must have spent quite a few days on the beach, for when he removed his sunglasses, I could see a pale mark running from his eyes to his ears. The rest of his skin was deeply tanned.

He came walking towards us. He was nearly as tall as Feluda and quite good-looking. He had a beard and a neatly trimmed moustache.

'I have heard of you,' he said. 'Are you already working on a case?'

'Why do you ask?'

'There's been a murder, I gather. So I thought you might be making inquiries.' Feluda laughed. 'No. I haven't been asked to investigate, so I couldn't make enquiries even if I wanted to.'

'You're staying at the Neelachal, aren't you?'

'Yes.'

'Er . . .' he seemed to be hesitating.

'Have you been appointed as guard?' Feluda asked. I had noticed it, too. The man was clutching three golden rings in his hand. He gave an embarrassed smile.

'It's such a bore . . . but you're right. These belong to a guest in my hotel. I met him only yesterday. This morning, he said he wanted to have a swim in the sea, but was afraid these might come off. So he asked me to hang on to them until he came out of the water. I wish I hadn't agreed.'

Before any of us could say anything, the owner of the rings arrived, dripping wet and accompanied by a *nulia*. We recognized him instantly. It was our 'golden' fellow passenger, Mr M.L. Hingorani. He saw Feluda and shouted, 'Good morning!' Then he took his rings back, and said 'Thank you' to the gentleman, adding that out of all the beaches he had seen in Goa, Miami, Acapulco and Nice, there was none like the beach in Puri.

We said goodbye to him and began walking again, this time accompanied by the bearded gentleman.

'I don't think I got your name—?' Feluda began politely.

'No, I didn't tell you my name, chiefly because I thought it might not mean anything to you. There is a special area in which I've made a small contribution, but not many would know about it. I am called Bilas Majumdar.'

Feluda frowned and looked at the man. 'Have you anything to do with mountains?' he asked.

'My God, your knowledge . . . !'

'No, no,' Feluda interrupted him, 'there's nothing extraordinary about this. It's just that I thought I had seen your name somewhere recently, in a journal or something. There was a mention of mountains in that report.'

'You're right. I joined the institute in Darjeeling to learn mountaineering. I am actually a wildlife photographer. I was supposed to go with a Japanese team to take photos of a snow leopard. You're probably aware that snow leopards can be found in the high altitudes of the Himalayas. Many have seen this animal, but there are virtually no photographs.'

We reached our hotel without further conversation. Lalmohan Babu kept casting admiring glances at Bilas Majumdar. Feluda ordered tea as soon as we got to our room. Mr Majumdar sat down and took out a photograph from his pocket.

'See if you can recognize this man,' he said to Feluda.

It was a postcard-size photograph. A man wearing a cap was holding a strange animal, and several others were looking at them both. The man Mr Majumdar was pointing at was someone we had just met.

'Yes, we left his house only a few minutes ago,' Feluda said. 'It's not easy to recognize him in that photo, since he's now got a beard.'

Mr Majumdar took the photo back. 'That's all I needed to know,' he said, 'I saw his name-plate outside his gate, but couldn't be sure if it was the same D.G. Sen.'

'That animal looks like a pangolin,' Feluda remarked.

Yes! Now I could remember having read about it. It was a species of anteater. It looked as though it was wearing a suit of armour.

'You're right, it is a pangolin. It's found in Nepal. That photo was taken outside a hotel in Kathmandu. D.G. Sen and I were both staying there.'

'When was this?'

'Last October. I had gone to meet that Japanese team. Some of my photos had been published in Japanese journals. When this team contacted me, I was naturally very excited. But, in the end, I couldn't go with them.'

'Why? Why?' Lalmohan Babu asked, sounding concerned. A mention of snow leopards had clearly made him smell an adventure.

'I had an accident. I was so badly injured that I had to spend three months in hospital.'

'Did your hurt your left leg?' Feluda asked.

'I broke the shin bone in my left leg. Why, is that

29

obvious from the way I walk?'

'No. But yesterday, we saw some footprints on the sand, and the mark left by a walking stick on the left side of these prints. So I thought whoever had come walking was either left-handed, or his left leg was injured. You, I can see, do not use a stick.'

'Sometimes I do. Walking on the sand can often be difficult. But I am only thirty-nine, you see. I don't feel like walking about with a stick in my hand all the time, like an old man.'

'Then it must have been someone else.'

'Perhaps. But I can tell you one thing. Breaking a shin bone was not my only injury. I had rolled down the side of a hill—nearly five hundred feet. A local farmer's son saw me fall on top of a tree—in fact, that's what saved my life—and informed a group of hippies. They took me to a hospital. I had seven broken ribs. Even my collar-bone was broken. There were injuries on my face, my chin was crushed. Eventually, I grew a beard simply to cover the marks on my chin. I lay unconscious for two days. When I came to, I could remember nothing, not even my name. Someone found my name and address in my diary and informed my family in Calcutta. A nephew came to see me. I couldn't recognize him. Then, gradually, my memory returned. Now, after a lot of treatment, I can remember most things, but not what happened just before the accident. For instance, my meeting with D.G. Sen was recorded in my diary, but it was only two days ago that I finally remembered what he looked like.'

'Can you remember why Mr Sen had gone to

Kathmandu? Was it anything to do with ancient manuscripts?'

'Manuscripts? Well, I don't know . . . what do these manuscripts look like?'

'Long, thin, and flat. About the size of a carton of cigarettes. They're usually covered by red silk.'

Mr Majumdar said nothing. His eyes were resting on a table lamp; he appeared to be lost in thought. All of us looked at him without saying a word. After a long time, he raised his eyes. 'I suppose I ought to tell you everything,' he said. 'The hotel in Kathmandu where Mr Sen and I stayed was called Vikram Hotel. It was a rather strange place. There were a few rooms with identical locks. You could use the key meant for one room to open the door of another, something which in a hotel one wouldn't expect at all. One day, purely by accident, I happened to unlock the room next to mine, thinking it was my own. It was, in fact, D.G. Sen's room. At first, I was surprised to find other people in what I thought was my own room, but soon I realized my mistake. So I quickly said "sorry" and came away, but not before I had seen something. D.G. Sen was sitting on the bed, and two strangers were sitting in chairs. One of them was taking out a thin, long packet from a cardboard box. As far as I can recall, it was red, though I couldn't tell you whether it was silk or not.'

'I see. What happened next?'

'Nothing. I mean, I can remember nothing. My mind's gone totally blank. The next thing I can remember is waking up in hospital.'

'Hey!' Lalmohan Babu exclaimed suddenly, 'Why

don't you go to the astrologer? He'll tell you everything, remind you of every detail.'

'Who are you talking about?'

'Laxman Bhattacharya the Great. He's a tenant on the ground floor of Mr Sen's house. I can make an appointment for you, if you like. Just try it out, it can't do any harm.'

'Well . . . that's an idea, anyway. Thanks.' Mr Majumdar seemed quite taken with the idea.

'All he'll do,' Lalmohan Babu continued, encouraged, 'is place his little finger on that mole in the middle of your forehead, and then he'll be able to see it all: your past, present, and future.'

I hadn't noticed it before, but now I saw a small mole on Mr Majumdar's forehead. It looked almost as though he was wearing a bindi.

'Does your astrologer allow visitors?' Feluda asked.

'Sure. You mean you and Tapesh would like to go as observers? No problem, sir. I'll tell him.'

'Very well. Please see if he's free at six o'clock this evening.'

Lalmohan Babu nodded happily, then told Mr Majumdar that the astrologer's fee was five rupees and seventy-five paise. Mr Majumdar started to laugh, but stopped when Feluda pointed out it wasn't a figure to be laughed at. 'Just think. If he gets even ten visitors every day, that gives him a monthly income of nearly two thousand rupees. That's not bad, is it?'

It was clear to me that although Feluda had no wish to have his future read, he was quite curious about the return of Mr Majumdar's memory.

CHAPTER 5

We decided to go to the famous temple of Jagannath in the evening before our meeting with Mr Bhattacharya. I was more interested in looking at the chariot. I had learnt from Feluda that every year, the old wooden chariot of Jagannath was broken methodically and a new one built in its place. Toys were made with the broken pieces of wood from the old one and sold in the market.

Feluda was not speaking much. Perhaps he was thinking of all the new people we had met and what they had said to us. There was one little thing that I felt I had to say to him.

'Have you noticed, Feluda,' I said, 'how everything seems to be related to Nepal? The man who got murdered was from Nepal, Bilas Majumdar went to Kathmandu, and so did D.G. Sen . . .'

'So? You think that has a special significance?'

'Well, yes, I mean . . .'

'There is no reason to assume anything of the kind. It's most probably no more than a coincidence.'

'OK, if you say so.'

Having seen the famous chariot, we were roaming around in the huge street market in front of the temple, looking at tiny statues and wheels of Konark being carved out of stone, when suddenly we bumped into Inspector Mahapatra. It took me a few seconds to recognize him, for he had had a haircut. One look at his new, freshly cropped hair reminded me of an uncle who always used to fall asleep the minute he sat in a barber's chair. When he woke up, the barber would show him his handiwork, which would invariably result in a violent argument. Inspector Mahapatra seemed to be a man who had a lot in common with my uncle.

'Hello, Inspector!' Feluda greeted him. 'Any progress? Did you manage to contact Mr Sarkar of Meher Ali Road?'

'We received some information this afternoon,' the Inspector replied. 'Fourteen Meher Ali Road is a block of apartments. There are eight apartments. Mr Sarkar lives in number 3. His flat's been locked for a week. Apparently, he goes out of town quite frequently.'

'Do you know where he's gone this time?'

'Puri.'

'Really? Who told you that?'

'The occupant in flat number 4. He's supposed to be here on holiday.'

'Did you get a description?'

'Yes, but it doesn't really mean anything. Medium height, clean-shaven, age between thirty-five and forty.'

'What does he do?'

'He calls himself a travelling salesman. No one seems to know what he sells. He took that flat a year ago.'

'And Rupchand Singh?'

'He arrived in Puri yesterday, and checked in at a hotel near the bus stand. He didn't even pay his bill. Last night, he had tried making a call from his hotel, but the phone was out of order. So he went to a chemist across the road and used their phone. The chemist saw him, but didn't hear what he said on the phone as he was busy serving his customers. Rupchand left the hotel at eleven, but did not return. We found a suitcase in his room with a few clothes in it. They were good clothes, well made and expensive.'

'That's not surprising. A driver these days earns pretty well. So I don't think Rupchand found it too difficult to be able to afford a few good things in life.'

Inspector Mahapatra left soon after this. We made our way to the Railway Hotel, where Mr Majumdar was waiting for us. We reached there at a quarter to six. The hotel had obviously been built during the British times. It had been renovated, but there was, even today, an old-fashioned air about it. In the large front garden, guests were drinking tea under garden umbrellas. Mr Majumdar rose from a table and came forward to meet us, with a brief 'Excuse me' to his companions.

'OK, let's go and find out what's in store,' he remarked.

Lalmohan Babu was our guide today. His whole demeanour had changed. When we reached Sagarika, he walked straight up the cobbled path and climbed on to the veranda, knocking the front door smartly. When no one appeared, he looked around just a little uncertainly, then pulled himself together and shouted 'Koi hai?' with a ring of such authority in his voice that we all looked at him in surprise. A side door opened instantly.

'Welcome!' said Laxman Bhattacharya. He was wearing a silk lungi and a fine cotton embroidered kurta. There was nothing remarkable in his appearance, except a thin moustache that drooped down, nearly touching the edge of his chin.

Lalmohan Babu began introductions, but was interrupted. 'Please come in,' Mr Bhattacharya invited, 'we can get to know each other when we're comfortably seated.'

We went into his sitting room, most of which was occupied by a large divan. This was probably where he worked. We took the chairs and stools that were strewn about. Apart from these, the room had no furniture. There was a built-in cupboard, the lower shelves of which were visible. Papers and wooden boxes had been crammed into them. There also appeared to be a few jars and bottles.

'Could you please sit here?' Mr Bhattacharya looked at Bilas Majumdar and pointed at the divan.

Mr Majumdar rose and took his place. Lalmohan Babu quickly introduced us. 'This is the friend I told you about,' he said, indicating Feluda, 'and the gentleman here is a famous wil—' he stopped, biting his lip. I knew he was about to say 'wildlife photographer', but had had the sense to check himself.

Feluda said hurriedly, 'I hope you don't mind two extra people in the room?'

'No, not at all. The only thing I do mind is being asked to perform on a stage. Many people have asked me to do that, as if I were a magician. Why, only this other—' Laxman Bhattacharya stopped speaking. I glanced at him quickly to find him staring at Bilas Majumdar. 'How very strange! You have a mole on the very spot where gods and goddesses have a third eye. Do you know what there is in the human body under that spot?'

'The pineal gland?' Feluda asked.

'Exactly. The most mysterious portion of the brain; or at least that's what western scientists say. Some thinkers in India are of the opinion that, thousands of years ago, most creatures, including man, had three eyes. In the course of time, the third eye disappeared and became the pineal gland. There is a reptile called Taratua in New Guinea that's still got this third eye.'

Feluda asked, 'When you lay a finger in the middle of one's forehead, is it simply to establish contact with the pineal gland?'

'Yes, you could say that,' Mr Bhattacharya replied. 'Mind you, when I first started, I hadn't even heard of this gland. I was only twelve at the time. One Sunday, an uncle happened to get a headache. "If you press my head," he said, "I'll give you money to buy ice-cream." So I began pressing his temples, and then he told me to rub his forehead. As I began running my finger on his forehead, pressing it gently, a strange thing happened. Scenes began to flash before my eyes—as though I was watching a film. I could see my uncle as a small boy, going to school; then as a young man, shouting "Vande Mataram" and being arrested by the police; then I saw him getting married, saw his wife's death, and even his own death. There he was before my eyes, lying with his eyes closed, surrounded by many other members of our family. Then the scenes disappeared as suddenly as they had appeared. I did not say anything to anyone, as I could hardly believe it myself. But when he did actually die and everything I had seen turned out to be true—well, I realized somehow I had acquired a special power, and . . .' his voice trailed away.

I looked at the others. Lalmohan Babu was gaping at Laxman Bhattacharya, round-eyed with wonder. Bilas Majumdar was looking straight at the astrologer, his face expressionless.

'I hear you have some knowledge about medicine, and I can see evidence of that in this room,' Feluda remarked. 'What do you call yourself? A doctor, or an astrologer?'

'Well, I did not actually learn astrology. To tell you the truth, my knowledge of stars and planets is quite limited. If I have the power to see a person's past and future, it is a God-given power. I myself have nothing to do with it. But ayurveda is something I have studied, as well as conventional medicine. So if you asked me what my profession was, I'd say I was a doctor. Anyway, Mr Majumdar, could you please come forward a little?'

Mr Majumdar slid forward on the divan, and sat cross-legged. The astrologer turned and dipped the little finger of his right hand into a little bowl, then wiped it with a spotless white handkerchief. I hadn't noticed the bowl before, nor could I tell what it contained. Whatever it was, it seemed to give Mr Bhattacharya sufficient encouragement to start his job. He closed his eyes, stretched his hand and placed his little finger on the mole on Mr Majumdar's forehead in a single, precise movement. After this, the next couple of minutes passed in silence. Nobody spoke. All I could hear was the ticking of a clock and the roaring waves outside.

'Thirty-three . . . nineteen thirty-three . . .' Mr Bhattacharya suddenly started speaking. 'Born under the sign of Libra . . . the first child. Tonsils removed at the age of eight—a scholarship—and a gold medal when leaving school—physics—a graduate at nineteen—started earning at twenty-three—a job—no, no, freelance—photography—struggle, I can see a lot of struggle—but great endurance and determination—love of animals—mountains—skill in climbing mountains—not married—travel a lot—not afraid to take risks . . .' he stopped.

Feluda was staring steadily at an ashtray. Lalmohan Babu was sitting straight, his hands clenched in excitement. My own heart was beating fast. Bilas Majumdar's face was still devoid of expression, but his eyes were fixed on the astrologer's face. Not for a single second had he removed them.

'Seventy-eight . . . seventy-eight . . .' the astrologer resumed speaking. Beads of perspiration stood out on his forehead. His breath came fast; he was obviously finding it difficult to speak.

'. . . Forest—there's a forest—the Himalayas—acci—acci—no, it's not.' He fell silent again, but only for a few seconds. Then he opened his eyes, and took his finger away. 'You,' he said, looking directly at Mr Majumdar, 'should not be alive today. Not after what happened. But you've been spared. God saved your life.'

'You mean it was not an accident?' Mr Majumdar's voice sounded choked. Laxman Bhattacharya shook his head, and helped himself to a paan. 'No,' he said, stuffing it into his mouth, 'as far as I could see, someone had pushed you deliberately down that hill. The chances of survival were practically nil. It's nothing short of a miracle that you didn't die on the spot.'

'But who pushed him?' Lalmohan Babu asked impatiently.

'Sorry,' Laxman Bhattacharya shook his head again, 'I couldn't tell you that. I did not see who pushed him. If I were to describe the person, or give you a name, it would be a total lie. And I would be punished for lying. No, I cannot tell you what I did not see.'

'Give me your hand, sir,' said Bilas Majumdar, offering his own. A second later, the photographer and the astrologer were seen giving each other a warm handshake.

We left soon afterwards.

CHAPTER 6

'What will you call this? Five-star, or six-star?' Feluda asked, looking at Lalmohan Babu.

We were having dinner at the Railway Hotel, at Mr Majumdar's invitation. 'I am very grateful to you,' he had said as soon as we had come out of Sagarika. 'Had it not been for you, I would not even have heard Laxman Bhattacharya's name. What he told me helped clarify a lot of doubts. In fact, I can even remember some of the details of what happened after that night when I walked into Mr Sen's room. So I'd be delighted if you could join me for dinner at my hotel.'

'I had no idea food in a railway hotel could be so good,' Lalmohan Babu freely admitted. 'I had assumed it would be as tasteless as what is served on trains. Now I know better, thanks to you.'

Bilas Majumdar smiled. 'Please have the souffle.'

'What? Soup plate? But I have already had the soup!'

'No, no. Souffle, not soup plate. It's the dessert.'

'Oh. Oh, I see.'

Mr Majumdar told us about the return of his memory while we all helped ourselves to the dessert.

'I was naturally embarrassed to have walked into someone else's room, but what I saw did not make me suspicious at all. Mr Sen was going to Pokhra the next day. He invited me to join him. The Japanese team I was waiting for was not expected for another three days. I had plenty of time, so I agreed. Pokhra is about two hundred kilometres from Kathmandu. We had to drive through a forest. Mr Sen asked the driver to stop there, to look for wild orchids. I got down with him, thinking even if we didn't find any flowers, I might get to see a few birds. I remember taking my camera with me. He went off in one direction to look for orchids. I went in another to look for birds.We decided to return to the car in an hour. I started to walk with my eyes on the trees, scanning every branch to see if I could find a bird. Suddenly, out of the blue, I felt a blow on my head, and everything went black.'

He stopped. We had already heard what followed next.

'You're still not sure about who had struck that blow?' Feluda asked.

'No, not at all. But I do know this: the car was parked on the main road, about a kilometre away, and I hadn't seen a single soul in that forest.'

'If the culprit was Mr Sen, you have no real evidence to prove it, have you?'

'No, I am afraid not.'

Lalmohan Babu seemed a bit restless, as though there was something on his mind. Now he decided to get it off his chest.

'Look,' he said, 'why don't you go and meet Durga Gati Sen? If he really is the man who tried to kill you, surely he'll think he's seeing a ghost? And surely that will give him away?'

'You're right. I thought of doing that. But there is a problem. You see, when he met me, I didn't have a beard. So he might not recognize me. Not instantly, anyway.'

We chatted for a few minutes before taking our leave. Mr Majumdar came up to the main gate to see us off. We set out, to discover that the sky was now totally clear and the moon had come out. Feluda had a small, powerful torch in his pocket, but the moonlight was so good that there was no need to use it.

We crossed over to the other side and began walking on the paved road that ran by the side of the sea. 'Tell me frankly, Felu Babu,' Lalmohan Babu said a few minutes later, 'what did you think of Laxman Bhattacharya? Isn't he incredible?'

'Incredible he might be, Lalmohan Babu. But what knowledge he has is not good enough. If Bilas Majumdar has to find out who had tried to kill him, he must come to me. It's Felu Mitter's brain that's required to discover the truth, not somebody's supernatural power.'

'You mean you're going to investigate?' Lalmohan Babu asked, his eyes glinting with excitement. Feluda opened his mouth to make a reply, but stopped as our eyes fell on a man, walking briskly towards us, staring at the ground and muttering to himself. It was Mr Hingorani.

He stopped short as he saw us. Then he shook a finger at Feluda and said, 'You Bengalis are very stubborn, very stubborn!' He sounded decidedly put out.

'Why?' Feluda smiled. 'What have we done to make you so annoyed?'

'That man refused. I offered him twenty-five thousand, and he still said no.'

'What! You mean there's actually someone in this world who could resist such profound temptation?'

'The fellow's mad. I had heard of his collection of manuscripts, so I made an appointment to go and see him. I said, "Show me your most valuable piece." So he opened a safe and brought out a piece going back to the twelfth century. An extraordinary object. God knows if it was stolen from somewhere. Last year, three old manuscripts were stolen from the palace museum in Bhatgaon. Two of them were recovered, but the third is still missing. It was one written by Pragya Paramita. So what I just saw might well have been the stolen one.'

'Where is Bhatgaon?' Lalmohan Babu asked. I had not heard of it either.

'Ten kilometres from Kathmandu. It's a very old town, used to be known as Bhaktapur.'

'But if it was stolen, he wouldn't have shown it to you, would he? And, as far as I know, there are plenty of manuscripts written by Pragya Paramita that are still

44

in existence,' Feluda remarked.

'I know, I know,' Mr Hingorani said impatiently. 'He said he bought it in Dharamshala, and it came to India with the Dalai Lama. Do you know how much he paid for it? Five hundred. And I offered him twenty-five thousand. Just imagine!'

'Does that mean your visit to Puri is going to be a total waste of time?'

'No. I do not give up easily. Mr Sen does not know this Mahesh Hingorani. He showed me another manuscript of the fifteenth century. I'm here for a couple of days. Let's see what happens. I don't usually take no for an answer. Well, good night to you all.'

Mr Hingorani went towards his hotel.

'It sounds a little suspicious, doesn't it?' Lalmohan Babu asked.

'What does?'

'This business of not wanting to sell something for twenty-five thousand rupees, when all he had bought it for was five hundred.'

'Why? Do you find it impossible to believe that a man can be totally devoid of greed? Did you know Uncle Sidhu refused to sell a manuscript from his own collection to Durga Gati Sen?'

'Why, Mr Sen didn't mention this!'

'That is what strikes me as most suspicious. He visited Uncle Sidhu only a year ago.'

Mr Sen was not just peculiar, but also rather mysterious, I thought. And if what Bilas Majumdar had said was true . . .

'But then,' Feluda continued, 'it isn't just Mr Sen my

suspicion's fallen on. Take your astrologer, for instance. The three-eyed reptile he told us about is called Tuatara, not Taratua; and it's not found in New Guinea, but New Zealand. Now, it's all right for Jatayu to make such mistakes. But if Laxman Bhattacharya's aim in life is to impress people with information like that, he really must learn to be more accurate. Then there's Nishith Bose. He has the awful habit of eavesdropping. He said Mr Sen suffers from gout. Those medicines in his room weren't for gout at all.'

'What were they for?'

'One of them was released only last year. I read about it in Time magazine. I can't quite recall what it's for, but it's certainly not for gout.'

'There's one other thing,' I put in, 'Mr Sen seemed amazingly preoccupied, didn't he? What's on his mind, I wonder? Besides, why did he say he didn't know his son?'

'No idea. I find it puzzling, too.'

'If it is true that he did try to kill Bilas Majumdar,' Lalmohan Babu said slowly, 'that could be a reason for his being so preoccupied. Maybe he is deeply worried. Maybe—'

He stopped. So did we. All of us stood staring at the ground.

There were footprints on the sand and, on the left, marks made by a walking stick. They were fresh marks, made in the last few hours.

Bilas Majumdar, who was likely to use a walking stick, had returned straight to his hotel from Laxman Bhattacharya's house to wait for us. He could not have come walking this way.

Who, then, had left these footprints?

Who else walked about on the beaches of Puri with a stick in his left hand?

CHAPTER 7

Lalmohan Babu's car arrived the following morning
just as we were planning to go out after breakfast.
His driver told us he had got held up in Balasore for
nearly four hours because of torrential rain, otehwise
he'd have reached Puri much sooner.

The Neelachal being full, we had booked a room
for the driver at the New Hotel, which was not far. He
left the car in the car park of our hotel, and went off to
find his own room. We told him we might go to
Bhubaneshwar later, weather permitting.

Feluda wanted to go to the station to buy a copy of
The Statesman. He wasn't satisfied with the Bengali
newspaper the hotel provided. Walking to the station
took us about half an hour. By the time we got there, it
was eight forty-five. The Jagannath Express from Calcutta
had arrived at seven. The Puri Express was late by an

hour, but it was expected any minute. I love going to railway stations, and to watch how a quiet and peaceful place can come to life and hum with activity when a train arrives.

Lalmohan Babu found a bookstall. 'Do you have books by the famous writer Jatayu?' he asked. There was, in fact, no need to do this since I could see at least three of his books displayed quite prominently. Feluda bought his newspaper and began leafing through some of the books. At this moment, we heard a voice. 'Has the latest *Mystery Magazine* arrived yet?' it asked. I turned to find Nishith Bose. He hadn't seen us at first, but when he did, he grinned from ear to ear. 'Just imagine, here I am buying the *Mystery Magazine*, when a detective is standing right next to me!' he exclaimed.

'How is your boss?' Feluda asked.

'Under great stress. People turn up without making an appointment, and then beg me to arrange a meeting. Who knew so many people were interested in old manuscripts?'

'Why, who else came visiting?'

'I don't know his name. He had a beard and he wore dark glasses. He said there was no point in giving his name, since Mr Sen wouldn't recognize it, but he knew someone who had some manuscripts to sell. So I went and informed Mr Sen, and he said all right, bring him up to the terrace. I showed him in, then went to my room to type a few letters. In less than three minutes, I heard Mr Sen calling my name. I ran to see what the matter was, and found him looking pale and greatly distressed, almost as though he was about to have a heart attack. All he could say to me was, "Take this man away, at once!" So I took him down the stairs immediately. He had the nerve to say before going, "I think your employer's heart isn't all that strong. Get him to see a doctor." Imagine!'

'How is he now?'

'Better, much better.' Mr Bose glanced at the clock and gave a start. 'Good heavens, I had no idea it was already so late. I must go now. You're going to be here for a few days, aren't you? I'll tell you everything one day. I have a lot to tell. Goodbye!'

The Puri Express had arrived while we were talking. The guard now blew his whistle and it began pulling out of the platform. Mr Bose disappeared in the crowd.

Feluda had selected a book from the stall and paid for it. I glanced over his shoulder and saw that it was called *A Guide to Nepal*. On our way back to the hotel, he said, 'I think it might be a good idea for you and Lalmohan Babu to go to Bhubaneshwar today. Something tells me I ought to remain here. I don't think anything drastic is going to happen very soon, but there's something in the air . . . I just don't like it. Besides, I need to sort a few things out. I must make a phone call to Kathmandu. Let's straighten all the facts out before they get too muddled.'

I was quite familiar with this mood Feluda was in. He would now withdraw himself totally and stop talking altogether. He would go back to his room and lie flat on his back, staring at the ceiling. When he did this, I had noticed in the past, sometimes he stared into space for three or four minutes without blinking even once.

Lalmohan Babu and I usually left him alone at a time like this or spoke in whispers. Going to Bhubaneshwar would be much better, I thought, than just hanging around waiting for Feluda to break his silence. I nodded at Lalmohan Babu, to indicate that we should leave as soon as possible.

We reached our hotel to find Mr Majumdar coming out of it.

'I'm so glad I've caught you!' he exclaimed. 'If you returned even a minute later, I'd have missed you.'

'Let's go upstairs.'

Mr Majumdar came into our room and sat down, wiping his face. 'You took my advice, didn't you?' Lalmohan Babu asked with a big smile.

'Yes. Mr Sen reacted exactly as you'd said he might. He jumped as though he'd seen a ghost. Amazing, isn't it, how he could recognize me despite this thick beard?'

'There is something very special in your face, Mr Majumdar, that your beard cannot hide,' Feluda pointed out.

'What?'

'Your third eye. It isn't easy to forget.'

'Yes, you're right. I forgot all about it. Anyway, something rather strange happened today. When I saw Mr Sen, I found a man who has aged dramatically in these few months. Why, he looks at least ten years older than what he had seemed in Kathmandu. I felt sorry for him. Yes, truly I did. Now I can put the whole thing behind me. If Mr Sen did try to kill me, I think he has paid for it already.'

'Good,' said Feluda, 'I am glad to hear this, for you

couldn't have got very far without concrete evidence, anyway.'

Mr Majumdar rose. 'What are your plans now?' he asked.

'These two are going to Bhubaneshwar today. I'll stay on here.'

'I think I'll leave Puri tomorrow. I haven't yet seen the forests of Orissa. I'll try and meet you again before I go.'

By the time we could leave, it was twelve-thirty. But it was a fine day, and the roads were good. Lalmohan Babu's driver drove at 80 kmph, which enabled us to reach Bhubaneshwar in exactly forty-two minutes. We went, first of all, to the temple called Raja Rani. A few years ago, the head of a *yakshi* carved on the wall of this temple had been stolen. Feluda had had to exercise all his brain power to get it back. It sent a shiver of excitement down my spine to see it back where it belonged.

There were dozens of other temples to be seen— Lingaraj, Kedar Gauri, Mukteshwar, Brahmeshwar and Bhaskareshwar, among others. Lalmohan Babu insisted on seeing each one because, he said, one of his school teachers—a very gifted man called Baikuntha Mallik— had written a poem on Bhubaneshwar that haunted him even today. Disregarding the presence of at least forty other tourists (many of them from abroad), he recited this poem for me in the temple of Mukteshwar:

On its walls
does Bhubaneshwar

tell the story of
  each sculptor.

Like Michaelangelo
  and Da Vinci,
all unsung heroes
  of our own country.

'It doesn't rhyme very well, does it?' I couldn't help saying, 'I mean, "Bhubaneshwar" hardly goes with "sculptor", and how can you rhyme "Da Vinci" with "country"?'

'Free verse, my boy, it's free verse!' Lalmohan Babu replied airily. 'It doesn't have to rhyme.'

We returned to Puri around seven in the evening. Bhubaneshwar was a nice place, neat and tidy, but I liked Puri much better because of the sea. Our manager, Shyamlal Barik, called out to us as we climbed the front veranda of the Neelachal.

'Mr Ganguli, there's a message for you!'

We went quickly to his room.

'Mr Mitter went out ten minutes ago. He told you to wait in your room.

'Why? What's happened?'

'There was a call from the police station. Mr D.G. Sen's house has been burgled. A very valuable manuscript has been stolen.'

How very strange! Feluda said only this morning he thought something might happen. Who knew it would happen so soon?

Chapter 8

A shower and a cup of tea refreshed me physically, but I felt too restless to sit still. Feluda had now officially begun his investigation. Puri, like so many other places we had gone to on holiday, had given us a mystery to work on. Knowing Feluda's calibre and his past performance, I was sure we would not go back disappointed.

But, I wondered, would Feluda get paid for his pains? After all, no one had actually hired him in this case. Not that it mattered. If the case was challenging enough and if he got the chance to exercise his brain, Feluda did not really care about money.

'Who do you suspect, Tapesh?' asked Lalmohan Babu. Unable to remain in his own room, he had joined me in mine and was pacing up and down, holding his hands behind him.

I said, 'Well, Nishith Bose had free access to the manuscripts, so he ought to be the prime suspect. But for that reason alone, I don't think he did it. Then there's Mr Hingorani. Didn't he say he wouldn't give up easily? And there's Bilas Majumdar. He might have stolen it to settle old scores. Maybe he couldn't bring himself to forgive and forget, after all. But Laxman Bhat—'

'No, no, no!' Lalmohan Babu interrupted, protesting violently, 'Don't drag Laxman Bhattacharya into this, please. He couldn't possibly be involved in theft. Why should he even dream of it? Just think of his special power!'

'Well then, what are your own views on this?' I asked him.

'I think the most important man is missing from your list.'

'Who?'

'Mr Sen himself.'

'What! Why should he steal his own property?'

'No, I'm not saying he stole anything. I mean, not this time. That manuscript was stolen, anyway, as Mr Hingorani said. So Mr Sen has sold it to him, for twenty-five thousand; and he's saying it's been stolen, to remove suspicion from himself. Don't you see, now if anyone asks for that particular manuscript, he has a valid reason for saying he hasn't got it?'

Could this be true? It seemed a bit far-fetched, but . . . I could think no further, for a room boy arrived at this moment and said there was a phone call for us. It had to be Feluda. I ran downstairs and took the call.

'Yes?'

'Did Mr Barik give you my message?' asked Feluda's voice.

'Yes. But have you been able to work anything out?'

'Mr Bose has disappeared.'

'Really? Who informed the police?'

'I'll tell you everything when I get back, in half an hour. How was Bhubaneshwar?'

'Fine. We—' I couldn't finish. Feluda had put the phone down.

I returned to my room and told Lalmohan Babu what Feluda had just said. He scratched his head and said, 'I would like to visit the scene of the crime, but I don't think your cousin would like that.'

We waited for another hour, but Feluda did not return. I began to feel rather uneasy. A little later, I ordered a fresh pot of tea, just to kill time. Then I did something Feluda had told me many times not to do. In my present state of mind, I simply could not help it. I opened his notebook and read the few entries he had made:

Diapid—gout—snake?—what will return?—why doesn't he know his son?—blackmail?—who?—why?—who walks with a stick?—

None of this made any sense. We waited for another twenty minutes, then our patience ran out. Lalmohan Babu and I left the hotel to look for Feluda. If he was going to return from Sagarika, we thought, he would probably take the road that ran by the sea. We turned right as we came out of the hotel.

As we began walking, it struck me once more how different the sea looked in the dark. The waves roared

with the same intensity as they did during the day, but
now they looked kind of eerie. It was the phosphorous
in the water that did it. How else could I have watched
them lashing the shore even under a cloudy sky? In the
far distance, the sky looked a shade brighter, possibly
because of the lights from the city. The rows of flickering
lights by the beach meant there was a colony of *nulias*.
Lalmohan Babu had a torch, but there was no need to
use it. My feet kept sinking in the sand. Lalmohan Babu
was wearing tennis shoes, but I had chappals on my
feet. Suddenly, one of these struck against something. I
stumbled and fell flat on my face. I must have cried out,
for Lalmohan Babu turned quickly with 'Why, Tapesh,
whatever—' A second later, he went through the same
motions and joined me on the ground. 'Help! Help!' he
cried hoarsely.

'Lalmohan Babu,' I whispered, 'I can feel something
under my tummy . . . I think it's a body, I can feel its
legs!'

'Oh, my God!' Lalmohan Babu managed to struggle
to his feet, pulling me up with him. Then he switched
his torch on, only to discover it wasn't working.

He turned it upside down and began hitting the
rear end in the hope of getting the batteries to work. At
this moment, a human figure slowly sat up on the sand.
I felt, rather than saw, it move.

'Give me your hand!' it said.

Feluda! Oh God, was it Feluda? Yes, it was.

I offered him my right hand. Feluda grabbed it and
stood up, swaying from side to side. Luckily, Lalmohan
Babu got the torch to work. He shone it briefly on

Feluda's face, holding it in an unsteady hand. Feluda raised a hand and touched his head, wincing in pain. When he brought his hand down, we could see, even in the dim light from the torch, that it was smeared with blood.

'D-did they c-crack open your sk-skull?' Lalmohan Babu stammered. Feluda ignored him. I had never seen him look so totally dazed.

'What happened? I can't imagine how—' he broke off, taking out a small torch from his own pocket. In its better and steadier light, we saw a series of footprints going from where he had fallen towards the high bank, where the sandy stretch ended.

We followed the footprints right up to the bank. Whoever it was had climbed over it and disappeared, but not without difficulty. There were clumps of uprooted grass strewn about, to prove that climbing had not been an easy task. There was nothing else in sight, not even a small *nulia* hut.

Feluda turned back to return to the hotel. We followed him.

'How long did you lie on the ground?' Lalmohan Babu asked, his voice still sounding strange. Feluda shone the torch on his watch and replied, 'About half an hour, I should think.'

'Shouldn't you see a doctor? That wound on your head may need to be stitched.'

'No,' Feluda said slowly. 'It is true that I received a blow on my head. But there is no injury, no open wound.'

'No? Then how did all that blood—?'

Lalmohan Babu's half-spoken words hung in the
air.

Feluda made no reply.

CHAPTER 9

Feluda placed an ice-pack on his head as soon as we reached our hotel. In half an hour, the swelling began to subside. None of us had any idea who might have hurt him. He was returning from Sagarika, Feluda said, when someone had flashed a powerful torch straight into his eyes, blinding him momentarily, and then knocked him unconscious. When he rang Mahapatra at the police station and reported the matter, Mahapatra said, 'You must take great care, Mr Mitter. There are a lot of desperate characters about. Why don't you stop your own investigation and let us handle this? Wouldn't that be safer?'

'If you had suggested this before I was attacked, I might have agreed. Now, Inspector, it is too late.'

When we came back to our room after dinner, it was nearly eleven. Rather unexpectedly, our manager,

Mr Barik, turned up, accompanied by another gentleman. 'He has been waiting for you for half an hour. I didn't want to disturb you while you were eating,' he said and returned to his room.

'I have heard of you,' the other man said to Feluda. 'In fact, having read about some of your past cases, I even know who your companions are. My name is Mahim Sen.'

Feluda frowned. 'That means—?'

'D.G. Sen is my father.'

None of us could think of saying anything for a moment. Mahim Sen went on, 'I came by car this afternoon. My company owns a guest house here. That's where I am staying.'

'Didn't you meet your father?'

'I rang him as soon as I got here. His secretary answered, and said after checking with my father that he did not wish to speak to me.'

'Why not?'

'I have no idea.'

'When I met your father recently, I got the impression that he wasn't very pleased with you. Can you tell me why?'

Mahim Sen did not reply immediately. He took out a packet of Rothmans from his pocket, and extracted a cigarette. He then lit it, inhaled and said, 'Look, I was never close to my father. I took no interest in his passion for manuscripts—I simply don't have the eye for art and antiques. I live in Calcutta and work for a private company. Sometimes I have to go abroad on business tours. But despite all this, I used to be on fairly good

terms with my father. If I wrote to him, he always replied
to my letters. I visited him twice with my family after he
moved to Puri, and spent a few weeks on the first floor
of his house. He was—and perhaps still is—extremely
fond of my eight-year-old son. But his behaviour on
this occasion just doesn't make any sense to me. I can
hardly believe that a strong man like him has gone senile
at the age of sixty-two. I do not even know if a third
person is responsible for this. So when I heard you
were in town, I thought I'd come and see you.'

'How long has your father had this secretary?'

'About four years. I saw him when I came in '76.'

'What kind of a man do you think he is?'

'That's difficult to say, I hardly knew him. All I can
say is that he may be good at keeping papers and files
in order and typing letters, but I'm sure my father
couldn't talk to him as he would to a friend.'

'Well then, you ought to know this: a most valuable
manuscript in your father's collection has been stolen,
and his secretary has vanished.'

Mahim Sen's jaw fell open.

'What! Did you actually go there?'

'Yes.'

'How did you find my father?'

'In a state of shock, naturally. Apparently, he has
recently started to sleep in the afternoon, and he takes
something to help him sleep. Today, an American was
supposed to meet him at half past six. Nishith Bose
had made this appointment. But, he wasn't there to
take this visitor up to meet your father. A servant met
him downstairs and accompanied him. Normally, Mr

Sen gets up by four o'clock, but today he slept till six. Anyway, he was up when this American arrived and said he wanted to take a look at the oldest manuscript. Your father then opened the safe in which it was kept, but discovered that, wrapped in red silk, were masses of white strips of paper. These were placed between two small wooden bars, so it was impossible to tell without unwrapping the packet that the real manuscript had gone. When he realized his most precious possession had been stolen, your father became so distressed that eventually the American visitor informed the police.'

'Does that mean it was Nishith Bose who—?'

'That's what it looks like. I met him this morning at the railway station. Now it seems he had gone to buy a ticket. The police made inquiries at the station, but by then, the Puri Express and other trains to Calcutta had left. They're still trying to trace him.'

Feluda stopped speaking. None of us knew what to say. Such a lot had happened in the last few hours— it made my head reel.

'Did you know your father had gone to Nepal last year?' Feluda asked.

'If he went after August, I wouldn't know, for I was abroad for seven months, starting from August. Father used to travel quite a lot to look for manuscripts. Why, what happened in Nepal?'

Feluda said nothing in reply, but asked another question instead.

'Are you aware that your father's got gout?'

Mahim Sen looked completely taken aback.

'Gout? My father's got gout? What are you saying, Mr Mitter?'

'Why, is that so difficult to believe?'

'Yes, it is. I saw Father last May. He used to go for long, brisk walks on the beach. He's always been careful with his diet, never drank or smoked, or done anything that might damage his health. In fact, he's always been rather proud of his good health. If what you're telling me is true, it's as amazing as it's tragic.'

'Could that be a reason for his present state of mind?'

'Yes, certainly. I don't think he could ever accept himself as an invalid.'

'Well, I am going to be here for a few days. Let's see what I can do. I must confess a lot of things are not clear to me,' Feluda said.

Mahim Sen rose. 'I came here to discuss a few things related to our old family business. I have to stay on until Father agrees to see me.'

He said goodbye after this, and left. We chatted for a while, then decided to go to bed. It was nearly midnight.

Lalmohan Babu stopped near the door and turned back. 'Felu Babu,' he said, 'I've just remembered something. You were supposed to ring Kathmandu, weren't you?'

'Yes, I was; and I did. I spoke to one Dr Bhargav in Veer Hospital, and asked him if anyone called Bilas Majumdar had been brought to this hospital last October with serious injuries.'

'What did he say?'

'He confirmed everything Mr Majumdar had told

us. There was a broken shin bone, a fractured collarbone, broken ribs and an injured chin.'

'Didn't you believe Mr Majumdar's story?'

'Checking and re-checking facts is an essential part of an investigator's job. Surely you're aware of that, Lalmohan Babu? Doesn't your own hero, Prakhar Rudra, do the same?'

'Y-yes, yes, of course . . .' Lalmohan Babu muttered and quickly left the room. I lay down, listening to the waves outside. I knew there was a similar turmoil in Feluda's mind. One thought must be chasing another, exactly like the restless waves of the sea, but he appeared calm, collected and at peace. When the *nulias* went into deep water in their fishing boats, past the breakers near the shore, perhaps that was what they got to see: a serene and tranquil sea.

'What is that, Feluda?' I asked, suddenly noticing a brown, square object Feluda had taken out of his pocket. A closer glance told me it was a wallet.

Feluda opened it and took out a few ten-rupee notes. Then he put them back and said absently, 'I found it in a drawer in Nishith Bose's room. He took his suitcase and his bedding, but left his wallet behind. Strange!'

CHAPTER 10

I opened my eyes the next morning to find Feluda doing yoga. This meant the sun wasn't yet up. He had been awake when I went to sleep the previous night, and had worked in the light of a table lamp until quite late. How he had managed to get up at the crack of dawn was a mystery.

A slight noise from the veranda made me glance in that direction. To my amazement, I saw Lalmohan Babu standing there, just outside his room, idly putting his favourite red-and-white Signal toothpaste on his toothbrush. Obviously, like us, he was too worked up to sleep peacefully.

Feluda finished his yoga and said, 'I'll have a cup of tea now, and then go out.'

'Where to?'

'Nowhere in particular. Just out. I need to clear my

brain. Sometimes looking at something enormous and colossal helps get things into perspective. I must stand before the sea and watch the sun rise. It may act like a tonic.'

By the time we finished our tea, many other guests in the hotel were awake, including Mr Barik.

Feluda went to see him before going out.

'Will you book another call to Nepal, please? Here's the number,' he said, 'and if Mahapatra calls, please tell him to leave a message. And—oh—are there good doctors here?'

'How many would you like? Of course we have good doctors here, Mr Mitter, you haven't come to a little village!'

'No, no, I know I haven't. But you see, I need a young and efficient doctor. Not someone doddering with age.'

'That's not a problem. Go to Utkal Chemist in Grand Road after ten o'clock. You'll find Dr Senapati in his chamber.'

Lalmohan Babu and I decided to go out with Feluda. The beach was deserted except for a few *nulia*s. The eastern sky glowed red. Grey clouds floated about, their edges a pale pink. The sea was blue-black; only the tops of the waves that crashed on the shore were a bright white.

The three *nulia* children we had seen on the first day were back on the beach, looking for crabs.

'The only minus point of this beautiful beach is those crabs,' Lalmohan Babu remarked, wrinkling his nose in disgust.

'What's your name?' Feluda asked one of the boys.
He had a red scarf wound around his head.

'Ramai,' he replied, grinning.

We walked on. Lalmohan Babu suddenly turned
poetic. 'Look at the sea . . . so wide, so big, so . . . so
liberating . . . it's hard to imagine there's been bloodshed
in a place like this!'

'Hm . . . blunt instrument . . .' Feluda said absently.
I knew murder weapons were usually of three kinds:
fire arms such as revolvers or pistols; sharp instruments
like knives and daggers; or blunt instruments such as
heavy rods or sticks. Feluda was clearly thinking of the
attack on him last night. Thank God it was nothing
serious.

'Footprints . . . look!' Feluda exclaimed suddenly. I
looked where he was pointing, and saw fresh marks:
footprints, accompanied by the now familiar mark left
by a walking stick.

'Bilas Majumdar! He must be an early riser,'
Lalmohan Babu observed. 'Do you really think so? Look
at that person over there,' Feluda said, pointing at a
figure in the distance. 'Do you think he looks like Bilas
Majumdar?'

It was not difficult to tell, even from a distance, that
the man who was walking with a stick in his left hand,
was not Mr Majumdar at all.

'You're right. It's someone else. Why, it's the
Sensational Sen!' Lalmohan Babu shouted.

'Correct. It's Durga Gati Sen.'

'But how come he's walking? What about his gout?'

'That's what I'd like to know. Perhaps Laxman

Bhattacharya's medicines can bring about miraculous recoveries, who knows?'

We resumed walking, each of us feeling puzzled. How many mysteries would we finally end up with?

The Railway Hotel emerged as we took a left turn. On our right I could see a few *nulias* and three foreigners clad in swimming trunks. One of them saw Feluda and raised a hand in greeting. Feluda waved back, explaining quickly that it was the same American who had informed the police from Mr Sen's house.

We walked on. There was Mr Hingorani, walking swiftly, with a towel flung over his shoulder. He was frowning darkly, looking most displeased. He didn't even glance at us. Feluda left the beach and began climbing up a slope. Something told me he was making his way to Sagarika. Had his brain cleared? Was he beginning to see the light? Before I could ask him anything, however, another voice piped up from somewhere. 'Good morning!' it said.

Laxman Bhattacharya was standing before us, wearing a lungi tucked in at the waist, a towel on his shoulder and a neem twig in his hand.

'Good morning. Where were you yesterday evening?' Feluda asked.

'Yesterday evening? Oh, I had gone to listen to some kirtan. There's a group in Mangalghat Road. They sing quite well. I go there every now and then.'

'You weren't home when I went looking for you. What time did you leave the house?'

'I can get away only after six. That's when I went.'

'I thought you might be able to shed some light on

69

this theft in Mr Sen's house, since you live in it yourself. It's possible to see the side lane from your room, isn't it?'

'Yes. In fact, I saw Nishith Bose leave with his luggage through that lane. This did not surprise me at the time, for he was expected to leave for Calcutta, anyway.'

'Really? Why?'

'His mother was seriously ill. He received a telegram the other day.'

'Did you see this telegram?'

'Yes, so did Mr Sen.'

'Why, he didn't say anything about it!' Feluda sounded surprised.

'Well . . . now, what can I say? You've seen for yourself the state he's in. He's destined to suffer. Who can change what's ordained?'

'Have you examined Mr Sen's future as well?' Lalmohan Babu asked anxiously.

'There are very few people in this town who haven't come to me. But do you know what the problem is? I cannot always tell people what I see. I open my mouth if I see symptoms of an illness. But how is it possible to say to someone things like: you'll one day commit a murder, or you'll go to prison, or you'll be hanged? No one will ever want to come to me if I told them such unpleasant things. So I have to choose my words very carefully because people wish to hear only good things.'

Mr Bhattacharya went off in the direction of the sea. We moved on towards Sagarika. It looked beautiful in the early morning sun.

'The house of death,' Lalmohan Babu said suddenly.

'How can you say that?' Feluda protested. 'You might call it the house of theft, but there hasn't been a death in this house.'

'No, no. I don't mean Sagarika,' Lalmohan Babu explained hastily. 'I mean this other house that looks like it might collapse any minute.'

We had seen this house before, but hadn't really noticed it in any detail. Sagarika was about thirty yards away from it. Now I looked at it carefully, and found myself agreeing with Lalmohan Babu. As it is, an old and crumbling building with damp, dank walls isn't a very pleasant sight. This building, in addition to all that, had sunk into the sand. Nearly six feet from the bottom was buried in the sand. This gave it a rather spooky air. I felt my flesh creep to look at it in broad daylight. What must it look like at night?

Instead of walking past it, Feluda walked into it today. The pillars of the front gate were still standing upright. There was a cracked and dirty marble slab that said 'Bhujanga Niwas'. If the house kept sinking, it wouldn't be long before the slab was submerged in sand. Beyond the gate there must once have been a small garden. A series of steps then led to a veranda. Only the top two steps were visible; others had disappeared in the sand. The railing around the veranda had worn away. It was surprising that the roof had not caved in. The room behind the veranda must have been a drawing room.

'It doesn't look totally abandoned,' Feluda remarked.

I saw immediately why he had said that, for, on the dusty floor of the veranda, were footprints.

'And there are matchsticks, Feluda!' I said. There were three matchsticks lying by a pillar.

'Yes, I guess if you tried to light a cigarette standing here in this strong wind, you'd be bound to waste a few,' Feluda replied.

We walked in through the gate. I was bursting with curiosity to go and find out what was inside the house. The door to the drawing room was open, rattling in the wind. Feluda inspected the prints on the floor. They were not very clear, for a fresh layer of sand had already settled over them. But there was no doubt that someone wearing shoes had walked on this veranda pretty recently.

Another thing became visible as Feluda removed some of the sand with his foot—a dark stain, which to me looked like paan juice. Lalmohan Babu, however, quickly stepped back and declared it had to be blood. Then he muttered something about it being time for breakfast. This clearly meant he had no wish to go into the house and would much rather go back to the hotel. I felt my own heart beating faster, partly in excitement and partly in fear. Only Feluda remained completely unperturbed. 'I think we ought to visit your house of death,' he announced, pushing the door gently. It swung open with a loud creak.

A musty, slightly foul smell wafted out immediately. Perhaps there were bats inside. It was totally dark in the room. If there were windows, they were obviously shut, and we ourselves were blocking the light coming in through the open door. Feluda crossed the threshold and stepped in. I followed him a second later. Only Lalmohan Babu hesitated outside. 'All clear?' he asked after a while in a voice that sounded unnaturally loud.

'Oh yes. And things will no doubt soon become even clearer. Come and see what's inside,' Feluda invited. By now my eyes had got a little focused in the dark, and I had seen what Feluda was referring to. There were a small trunk and a bedding, wrapped carelessly in a durrie. Both had been dumped in a corner.

'The police are wasting their time,' Feluda said slowly. 'Nishith Bose has not gone to Calcutta.'

'Well then, where is he?' Lalmohan Babu asked, surprised. He had finally joined us in the room.

Feluda did not reply.

'Hmm. Very interesting,' he muttered, staring at something else. I followed his gaze. In another corner was a small heap, consisting of long, narrow pieces of wood and reams and reams of cheap yellow paper, tied with strings.

'Any idea what this might mean?' Feluda asked.

'Those pieces of wood . . . why, they look like the wood used for manuscripts!' Lalmohan Babu exclaimed. 'And . . . oh!' He seemed bereft of speech.

'It seems Nishith Bose had started a regular factory,' I said slowly, 'for making fake manuscripts. I guess all he had to do was chop bits of wood down to the right size, then place bits of paper between them, and wrap the whole thing up in red silk. It would certainly have looked like an ancient manuscript.'

'Exactly,' said Feluda. 'It is my belief that many of

Mr Sen's manuscripts are fake. What he had bought was genuine, of course, but since then someone has removed the original piece and replaced it with plain paper. The real stuff has been sold to people like Hingorani.'

'Oh, ho, ho, ho!' Lalmohan Babu suddenly found his tongue. 'Remember that strip of paper I saw on our first visit to Mr Sen's house? The one I thought was a snake? That must have been a piece of paper used for making dummies of real manuscripts.'

'Undoubtedly,' Feluda said firmly.

We were standing in the middle of the room. There were two side doors, one on our right and the other on our left. Presumably, they led to other rooms. Through the open front door—through which we had walked a few minutes ago—a strong sea breeze blew in with considerable force. The door to our right opened unexpectedly, making a loud noise that sounded almost like a gunshot. What followed next froze my blood. Even now, my heart trembles as I write about it.

Lalmohan Babu was the first to look through the open door. He made a strange noise in his throat, his eyes began popping out, and he'd probably have fainted; but Feluda leapt forward and caught him before he could sink to the floor. In speechless horror, I stared at the figure that lay on the floor in the next room. It was a man. No, it was the dead body of a man; and even I could tell he had lain there, dead, for quite some time, although his eyes were still open. I had no difficulty in recognizing him.

It was D.G. Sen's secretary, Nishith Bose.

CHAPTER 11

Feluda had to miss breakfast that day.

Once Lalmohan Babu had recovered somewhat, we went to the Railway Hotel as it was closer and rang the police from there. Then we returned to our own hotel.

Feluda left us soon afterwards. 'I have a few things to do, particularly in the *nulia* colony, so I've got to go,' he said. He had already told us—even without touching the body—that Mr Bose had been killed with a blunt instrument, though there was no sign of the weapon. Who knew when Lalmohan Babu had called the broken old Bhujanga Niwas the 'House of Death', he was actually speaking the truth?

There was, however, a piece of good news. D.G. Sen and his son appeared to have got back together. While coming out of Bhujanga Niwas, I happened to glance at Sagarika and saw both father and son on the roof. Mahim Sen gave us a cheerful wave, so presumably all was well. How this sudden change in their relationship had occurred, I could not tell. It was most mystifying.

Feluda returned at a quarter to eleven. I suddenly remembered he had booked a call to Nepal. 'Did your call come through?' I asked.

'Yes, I just finished speaking.'

'Did you call Kathmandu?'

'No, Patan. It's an old town near Kathmandu, on the other side of the river Bagmati.'

'Felu Babu,' Lalmohan Babu squeaked, 'I can't get over the shock. Look, I am still shivering.'

'Do stop, Lalmohan Babu. At least, save some of it for tonight.'

'Why—what is happening tonight?'

'Tonight,' Feluda replied calmly, 'we'll have to stand—not on one leg, mind you—but stand still and wait.'

'Where?'

'You'll see.'

'Why? What for?'

'You'll learn, by and by.'

Lalmohan Babu opened his mouth once more, then shut it, looking crestfallen. But then, like me, he wasn't unfamiliar with the kind of mood Feluda was in. One could ask him a thousand questions, but he wouldn't give a straight answer.

'Dr Senapati is quite a smart young doctor,' Feluda said, changing the subject.

'Why, have you been to his clinic already?' I asked.

'Yes. He has been treating Mr D.G. Sen. He went to America last April. It was he who brought that medicine.'

'Diapid?' The name had got stuck in my memory for some reason.

'Since you ask, I can tell you'll never need to use it yourself,' Feluda laughed. God knows what this cryptic remark meant. I didn't dare ask.

Inspector Mahapatra rang an hour later. The police surgeon had finished his examination. According to him, Nishith Bose had been killed between 6 and 8 p.m. last evening, with a blunt instrument. There was still no sign of the weapon. But the police had found traces of blood under the sand below the veranda. Presumably, the murder took place near the front gate. Mr Bose's body was then dragged inside.

A sudden idea flashed through my mind, but I chose not to say anything to Feluda. Could it be possible that whoever killed Mr Bose had attacked Feluda, using the same instrument? Perhaps that was why there was blood on his head, even without an open wound?

At around half past twelve, I began to feel hungry. Lalmohan Babu, too, started to comment on the heavenly smell emanating from the kitchen. But, at this moment, Bilas Majumdar turned up.

'Would you like to go?' he asked without any preamble.

'Where to?' Feluda asked, busily scribbling something in his notebook.

'A place called Keonjhargarh, in an airconditioned limousine supplied by the tourist department. There's room for six. But I found only one other person to go with me, an American called Steadman. He's a wildlife enthusiast as well. You'll find it interesting, I'm sure, if you come with us.'

'When are you leaving?'

'Straight after lunch.'

'No, thank you. I'm afraid I've got some work this afternoon. In fact, if you could stay back for a few hours, I might be able to show you a sample of the wildlife in Puri!'

'No, Mr Mitter, thank you very much.' Mr Majumdar smiled and left.

A minute later, we heard a heavy American car start. Then it turned around and sped towards the north.

When was the last time I had been under such tense excitement? I couldn't remember.

We had dinner at nine that evening. An hour later, Feluda announced it was time to go. 'You'll have to be suitably dressed,' he told me. 'Don't wear kurta-pajamas, and don't wear white. I don't need to tell you what you must wear to hide in the dark, do I?'

No, there was no need to do that, I thought, my mind going back to our experience in the graveyard in Park Street.

'My instincts tell me something is going to happen tonight,' Feluda added, 'but there is no guarantee that it will. So prepare yourselves for possible disappointment.'

I looked at the sky as we went out, and saw that

there were no stars. Lalmohan Babu, who had formed a habit of looking up at the sky every now and then (not in search of stars or the moon, but for signs of the skylab), quickly raised his head and said, 'Had the wind been blowing in a different direction, the pieces might have fallen into the sea. Now . . . anything can happen.'

Although Bhujanga Niwas was surrounded by sand, the actual beach was about fifty yards away from it. There were a few makeshift shelters where the beach started, presumably for the guests in the Railway Hotel who came to bathe in the sea. Large reed mats had been fixed over bamboo poles to create these shelters. Feluda stopped beside one of these. Behind us was the sea, still roaring loudly, but now hardly visible in the dark. If anyone went walking past our shelter, we'd be able to see his figure, but we might not recognize him. There was no chance of being seen ourselves. Feluda could not have chosen a better spot in which to hide. It was still not clear why we were hiding, and I knew he wouldn't tell me even if I asked. Annoyed with his habit of keeping things to himself, Lalmohan Babu had once said to him, 'You, Felu Babu, should make suspense films. People would die holding their breath. Much better than even Hotchkick, that would be!'

I could see Mr Sen's house from where we were standing. The light in his room on the second floor was still on. A light on the first floor had just gone out. Only one window on the ground floor was visible over the compound wall. A light was on, so perhaps Laxman Bhattacharya was still awake.

We were all sitting on the sand under the shelter,

in absolute silence. Speaking would have been difficult, in any case, because of the noisy waves. By now my eyes had got used to the darkness and I could see a few things. On my left was Lalmohan Babu. The few remaining strands of hair around his bald head were blowing hard in the strong wind, rising like tufts of grass. Feluda sat on my right. I saw him raise his left hand and peer at his wrist. Then he slipped his hand into his shoulder bag and took out an object—his Japanese binoculars.

He placed it to his eyes. I knew what he was looking at. D.G. Sen was standing near his open window. After a few moments, he moved aside and picked something up with his right hand.

What was it?

Oh, a glass tumbler. What was he drinking from it?

The light on the ground floor had gone out. Now Mr Sen switched off his own light. Immediately, the darkness around us seemed to grow more dense. However, I could still vaguely see my companions, especially if they made a movement.

Lalmohan Babu took out his torch from his pocket. I quickly leant over and whispered in his ear: 'Don't switch it on!' In reply, he turned his head and muttered: 'This is a blunt instrument. It may come in handy, even if I don't switch it on.' He moved his head away; and, at this moment, I saw something that made my heart fly into my mouth. On our right, about ten yards away, was another shelter. A man was standing next to it. God knows when he had appeared. Lalmohan Babu had seen him, too. He dropped the torch in astonishment.

And Feluda?

He hadn't seen him. He was looking straight at Sagarika. I forced myself to look in the same direction, and spotted instantly what Feluda had already seen.

A man was walking out of Sagarika. Was he going to come towards us? No. He made his way to the broken and abandoned Bhujanga Niwas. He slowed down as he got closer to the building, then stopped near one of the pillars. What was he going to do?

It became clear in the next instant. A second man appeared from behind the house and joined the first. There were now two male figures standing before the gate. It was impossible to tell if they spoke to each other, but they separated in a few seconds and started to walk in different directions. The one who had come from Sagarika was making his way back—!

On no! Lalmohan Babu had jabbed at his torch carelessly and switched it on by accident. Feluda snatched it from his hand and threw it down on the sand. But, in the same instant, someone fired a gun. A bullet came and hit one of the bamboo poles of our shelter, making an ear-splitting noise and missing Lalmohan Babu's neck by a few inches.

'Get the other one!' hissed Feluda and shot up like a rocket to chase the second man. To my own surprise, I discovered that those few words from Feluda were enough to make me forget fear. I jumped to my feet without a word and began sprinting towards the first man.

It did not take me long to catch up with him. I threw

myself at his legs, a bit like a rugby player doing a 'flying tackle', and managed to grab them both. The man tripped and fell flat on his face. I lost no time climbing on to his back. Then I looked around for Feluda.

Two silhouettes were standing at a slight distance, facing each other. I saw one of them raise a hand and aim for the other's chin. A second later, the second figure was knocked down on the ground. I even heard the faint thud as he fell.

In the meantime, Lalmohan Babu had joined me and was dancing around with his blunt instrument in his hand, waiting for a suitable opportunity to strike the figure wriggling under me. However, another soft thud soon told me that, in his excitement, he had dropped his weapon on the sand once more.

'Bring him over here!' Feluda shouted.

This time, Lalmohan Babu was of real help. He took one leg, and I caught the other. Together, we dragged the man to join Feluda. Feluda was standing with one foot on the chest of his opponent, and the other on his right hand. The revolver this hand had held a few moments ago was lying nearby.

'Until today, you had no injury on your chin. But after this, I think there will be a permanent mark,' Feluda declared solemnly, shining his pocket torch on the man.

The word 'wildlife' suddenly flashed through my mind. Pinned down by his feet, staring back at Feluda, his eyes wild with anger, was Bilas Majumdar. His left hand was still curled around an object wrapped in red silk. Another manuscript! Feluda bent down and snatched it away. Then he turned and shone his torch on our prisoner. 'What is your third eye telling you, Laxman Babu?' Feluda asked, 'Did you know what was written in your own destiny?'

Suddenly, several shadows emerged from the darkness. Who on earth were these people?

'Hello, Mr Mahapatra,' Feluda greeted one of them, 'I'm going to hand these two culprits over to you, but I haven't yet finished. I'd like us all to go and sit in the living room of Bhujanga Niwas. These two men must come with us.'

Four constables stepped forward and grabbed Bilas Majumdar and Laxman Bhattacharya. 'Mahim Babu, are you there?' Feluda called.

'Oh yes. Here I am!' Mahim Sen raised a hand. With a start, I realized he was the man we had first seen standing near a shelter. 'I think Father's about to join us. Look, there he is, with a torch,' he added, pointing.

'We've made seating arrangements in the front room of that building,' said Mr Mahapatra, pointing at Bhujanga Niwas. 'There will be room for all, don't worry.'

'Why, it's just fine outside, why not—?' began Lalmohan Babu, but I don't think anyone heard him, for everyone had already started walking towards Bhujanga Niwas.

CHAPTER 12

'Come in, Mr Sen, we're all waiting for you,' Feluda opened the door. Mahim Sen came in with his father. Three lanterns had been lit in the room, the police had clearly worked quite hard at cleaning and dusting. It looked a different room altogether.

Father and son took two chairs.

'Here's your *Kalpasutra*,' said Feluda, offering him the manuscript he had just recovered from Bilas Majumdar. Mr Sen looked visibly relieved as he took it, but asked with considerable anxiety, 'What about the other one?'

'I am coming to that. You'll have to bear with me. I hope you didn't take a sleeping pill today?'

'No, no, of course not. That's what led to this disaster. God knows what he put in my glass of water yesterday!' Mr Sen glared at Laxman Bhattacharya.

'What I fail to understand is why you went to this humbug in the first place. Didn't you know there were other much better doctors in town?'

'I did, Mr Mitter. But he came to me himself, and everyone else said he was very good. So I thought I should give him a chance. Besides, he said he knew of old manuscripts and scrolls . . . he could get me a few . . .'

'That's your biggest weakness, isn't it? And he took full advantage of it. Anyway, I hope the Diapid has worked? That's supposed to be the best among modern drugs to bring back lost memory.'

'It's worked like a charm!' Mr Sen exclaimed. 'My memory is coming back to me, exactly as if one door is being opened after another. Thank God Dr Senapati came to me himself and gave me that medicine. You see, I had even forgotten that it was he who used to treat me before!'

'Well then, tell me, Mr Sen, can you recognize this gentleman?' Feluda flashed his torch on Bilas Majumdar. Mr Sen stared at him for a few seconds, then said slowly, 'Yes, I could recognize him yesterday from the look in his eyes and his voice. But still, I wasn't sure.'

'Can you remember his name?'

'Certainly. But he may have changed it here.'

'Is his name Sarkar?'

'Yes, that's right. Mr Sarkar. I never learnt his first name.'

'Liar!' Mr Majumdar screamed. 'Do you want to see my passport?'

'No, we don't,' Feluda's voice was ice-cold. 'A criminal like you may well have a fake passport. That won't mean anything at all. What's in it, anyway? It describes you as Bilas Majumdar, right? And states that you have a distinguishing mark on your forehead, a mole? OK. Now watch this.'

Feluda strode over to Mr Majumdar and took out his handkerchief from his pocket. Then, without any warning whatsoever, he struck at his forehead with the handkerchief still in his hand. This made the false mole slip out and hit the dark floor.

'You made a lot of inquiries about Bilas Majumdar, didn't you?' Feluda went on. 'You knew he had gone to take photos of a snow leopard, and then he had had an accident. You even knew which hospital he had been taken to, the nature of his injuries and that he had been kept in the same hospital until last month. But a tiny news item escaped your notice. I had read it, but hadn't paid much attention at the time. Yesterday, Dr Bhargav of Veer Hospital in Kathmandu confirmed what I vaguely remembered having read. Bilas Majumdar's most serious injury was to the brain. He died three weeks ago.'

Even in the dim light from the lanterns, I could see the man had turned white as a sheet. 'Listen, Mr Sarkar,' Feluda said, 'your profession is something that no passport will ever reveal. You are a smuggler. Perhaps you don't always steal things yourself, but you certainly help in transferring smuggled goods. In Kathmandu, you had come upon the scroll stolen from the palace museum in Bhatgaon. Mr Sen will tell you the rest.'

The look in D.G. Sen's eyes was cold and hard as steel. He said, 'This man and I happened to be staying in the same hotel in Kathmandu. One day, I unlocked his door by mistake, and found two other men in his room. One of them was in the process of handing him an object wrapped in red silk. I realized immediately that it was a manuscript. But all I could do at that moment was apologize and come away. God knows what happened to me that night. When I woke up, I found myself in a hospital. Every memory prior to this incident was gone from my mind. But people were very kind. They found my address from the hotel, and eventually managed to inform my family. Nishith went and brought me back. I had to spend three and a half months in hospital.'

'I think I can fill the gaps in your memory. If I get anything wrong, perhaps Mr Sarkar will correct me?' Feluda said coolly. 'You were obviously given something that made you unconscious. You were then taken by car outside the main city, into the mountains and dropped from a height of five hundred feet. Mr Sarkar was convinced you were dead. However, nine months later, when he came to Puri to transfer the stolen scroll, he saw your nameplate and began to get suspicious. It is my belief that the occupant of your ground floor, Mr Laxman Bhattacharya, supplied him with all the necessary information regarding your present condition. Am I right?'

Laxman Bhattacharya, who had not uttered a single word so far, burst into speech at this. 'What are you saying, sir? I supplied all the information to him? Why, I saw him for the first time when you brought him to my place!'

'Really?' Feluda walked across to stand directly before Laxman Bhattacharya. 'Well then, Mr Astrologer, tell me this: when we took him to your place, you asked him to sit on the divan immediately, and told us to take the chairs. How did you know he was Bilas Majumdar, and not me? Who told you that?'

Laxman Bhattacharya could not make a reply. He seemed to shrink into himself with just that one question from Feluda.

Feluda continued. 'I think the idea of stealing manuscripts first occurred to Mr Sarkar when he heard about Mr Sen's loss of memory, and when Laxman Bhattacharya offered to help him. He knew he could easily find a buyer for an old and valuable scroll, since Mr Hingorani was in the same hotel. But three major difficulties suddenly arose to complicate matters. Firstly, a totally undesirable character followed Mr Sarkar all the way to Puri. It was Rupchand Singh. He really gave you a lot of trouble, didn't he? I mean, it's easy enough to bribe the driver of a car that takes an unconscious man to the top of a hill to kill him. But what happens if this driver is not happy with what he has been paid? What if he's greedy and starts blackmailing you to get more? What can anyone do under such circumstances, tell me, but kill the blackmailer?'

'Lies, lies, lies!' Mr Sarkar cried desperately.

'Suppose, Mr Sarkar, I could prove that the bullet that killed Rupchand Singh had come from your own revolver? This same revolver you had tried to use on us a little while ago? What then?'

Mr Sarkar sank back instantly. I could see that his

whole body was bathed in sweat. I was sweating, too, but that was simply in breathless excitement. Lalmohan Babu, sitting next to me, was looking as though he was watching a fencing match. It was true, of course, that Feluda's words were as sharp as a sword; and the game wasn't over yet.

'Rupchand Singh was victim number one,' Feluda continued. 'Now let's look at the second problem Mr Sarkar had to tackle. It was my own arrival in Puri. Mr Sarkar realized he could do nothing without somehow pulling the wool over my eyes. So he decided to pass himself off as Bilas Majumdar. I must say initially he succeeded very well in this task. Not only that, he even managed to shift his own blame on to an old man who had lost his memory. It was this initial success that made him a bit reckless. His plan was quite simple. If he could get hold of a manuscript, he'd sell it to Hingorani. There was no way he could get it from its rightful owner, for Mr Sen wasn't even remotely interested in money, and the old manuscripts to him were perhaps more precious to him than his own life. So the stuff had to be stolen from the safe. How would he do that? Very simple. The job would be done by Laxman Bhattacharya, because he had been doing it for quite sometime. When he did it before, he had obviously pocketed the whole amount himself. In this particular case, he agreed to share with Mr Sarkar the money Hingorani offered, since it was a fairly large sum. But they had to consider one other person. It was Mr Sen's secretary, Nishith Bose.'

Feluda paused. Then he walked over to Mr Bhattacharya once more and asked, 'Didn't you say something about going to a kirtan?'

Laxman Bhattacharya tried to appear nonchalant. 'So I did,' he said. 'Why, you think I lied?'

'No. You didn't lie about the kirtan. It is true that a group of singers get together every Monday for a session of kirtan. But you have never gone there. I checked. However, there was one person who used to go there regularly. It was Nishith Bose. He used to be absent from his duties every Monday from five to six-thirty in the evening. A servant used to be around at that time to take care of visitors. He was bribed last Monday, after Mr Bose left the house. You, Mr Bhattacharya, tampered with Mr Sen's glass of water, got him to take a heavy dose of your sleeping pills, and then entered his room at five-thirty. Then you took the key from under his pillow, opened the safe and removed one of the most precious manuscripts, in order to hand it over to Mr Sarkar. You had arranged to meet him on the veranda of this house. You arrived here first, and spent some time waiting for your accomplice. Your footprints, your used matchsticks and the paan juice you spat out on the floor, all gave you away. But something totally unexpected happened while you were waiting, didn't it, Mr Bhattacharya?'.

Laxman Bhattacharya made no attempt to speak. He was trembling violently, as—with the only exception of Mr Sarkar—everyone in the room was staring at him. I felt my body go rigid with tension.

Feluda started speaking again.

'An American was supposed to visit Mr Sen at half-past six that evening. So Nishith Bose returned at six, which was much earlier than usual. Perhaps he started to get suspicious when he found his employer still asleep. He must then have opened the safe and discovered the theft. You were not at home. This must have made him even more suspicious. So he came out of the house, saw your footprints on the sand, and followed you to Bhujanga Niwas. When you realized you had been caught red-handed, what could you do but finish Mr Bose instantly? You had a blunt instrument in your hand, didn't you? So you used it to kill Mr Bose, then removed his body and returned to Sagarika to fetch his suitcase and bedding. Just as all seemed to be well, you saw that there were blood stains on your weapon. So you left once more to throw it into the sea, but who did you run into on your way to the beach? It was me. You struck my head with the same weapon, and then dropped it in the water. Tell me, is any of this incorrect?'

Feluda stopped, although he must have known Laxman Bhattacharya was totally incapable of making a reply. But the brief pause helped in emphasizing his next question. It shot through the air like a bullet.

'In spite of all this, Mr Bhattacharya, could you get what you wanted?'

Silence. Feluda answered his own question. 'No. Hingorani didn't get that scroll, nor did Mr Sarkar. That was why you found it necessary to steal the second most valuable manuscript tonight. By this time, you had told everyone the story about Mr Bose's mother's illness which accounted for his absence. But can you tell these people now why you failed to get the first manuscript? No? Very well, I'll tell them, for I don't think you could explain the details of such an extraordinary occurrence. Even I was fooled at first. I've solved a number of difficult cases, but this one was truly amazing. I knew the instrument used was a blunt one, but how was I to know it was the scroll itself? Yes, the stolen scroll, written by Pragya Paramita in the twelfth century. How was I to know that that was the only thing Laxman Bhattacharya had in his hand to strike a person with? I couldn't figure it out, despite being hit by the same wooden bars. The scroll was bloodstained. Some of that blood got smeared on my own head. Naturally, you could not pass it on to either Sarkar or Hingorani.'

'Oh no, oh no, oh no!' cried D.G. Sen, covering his face with his hands. 'My manuscript! My most precious, my very—'

'Listen, Mr Sen,' Feluda turned to him. 'Did you know that the sea doesn't always accept what's offered to it? In fact, sometimes, it returns an offering almost immediately?'

Feluda slipped a hand into his shoulder bag and, almost like a magician, brought out a manuscript covered in red silk.

'Here is your *Ashtadashasahasrika Pragya Paramita*. The silk wrapper is quite unharmed. The wooden bars have been damaged, but the actual writing is more or less unspoilt. Not much water could seep in through layers of wood and cloth.'

'But . . . but . . . where did you get it, Felu Babu?' Lalmohan Babu gasped.

'You saw that piece of red silk this morning,' Feluda replied. 'That little *nulia* boy called Ramai was wearing it round his head. It made me think. That's why I went to the *nulia* colony and retrieved it. Ramai had found the scroll stuck in the wet sand near the edge of the water. He took the silk wrapper, but the manuscript was kept safe in his house. I had to pay ten rupees to get it. Mr Mahapatra, will you please get Sarkar's wallet and give me ten rupees from it?'

I had no idea the sea looked so much more enormous from the terrace of Mr Sen's house. I stood near the railing, marvelling at the sight.

Last night, after the police had left with the two culprits, Mr Sen had invited us for morning coffee. Mahim Sen had spent the night with his father, since Nishith Bose was dead and the servant had run away. On hearing this, Feluda offered immediately to speak to Shyamlal Barik of our hotel and arrange for a new servant. The cook brought us coffee on the terrace.

By this time, Mr Sen had handed a cheque to Feluda. The amount on it was so handsome that it made up for all the weeks Feluda had spent at home before coming to Puri. Initially, Feluda had refused to accept it, but when Mr Sen began to insist, he had to take it. Lalmohan Babu said to him later, 'If you didn't take that cheque, Felu babu, I would have hit you with a blunt instrument. Why do you turn all modest and humble when you're offered payment? I find it most annoying!'

'Do you know, Mr Sen,' said Feluda, sipping his coffee, 'what baffled me the most? It was your gout.'

Mr Sen raised his eyebrows. 'Why? What's so

THE ADVENTURES OF FELUDA

baffling about that? Can't an old man get gout?'

'Yes, but you go for long walks on the beach, don't you? I saw your footprints on the sand but, like an idiot, thought they were Majumdar's—I mean, Sarkar's. But yesterday, I realized it was you.'

'So what did that prove? Gout is extremely painful, but the pain does sometimes subside, you know.'

'I'm sure it does. But your footprints tell a different story, Mr Sen. I didn't raise this last night because I thought you wanted to keep it a secret. The trouble is, you see, it isn't always possible to keep secrets from an investigator. The stick you use is pretty significant, isn't it? Besides, your shoes aren't both of the same size. I noticed that.'

Mr Sen sat in silence, looking straight at Feluda. Feluda resumed speaking. 'The Veer Hospital in Kathmandu confirmed the news about Bilas Majumdar's accident. But no one else had been brought there with similar injuries. Then I looked at my guide book and realized that there was another hospital called Shanta Bhavan in Patan, which is near Kathmandu. I rang them, and was told that one Durga Gati Sen had been brought there with severe injuries in October last year. He remained there until early January. They even gave me the details of those injuries.'

The expression on Mr Sen's face changed. He sighed after a short pause, and said, 'Nishith knew I didn't want anyone to learn about what had happened. If I had visitors in the morning, he always dressed my foot with a fresh bandage and told them I had gout. Today, Mahim has done this job. I certainly did not want this fact publicized, Mr Mitter. What happened to me was no less tragic than losing an ancient and valuable manuscript. But since you have already guessed the truth . . .'

He raised his trousers to expose his left leg.

To my complete amazement, I saw that the dressing finished three inches above his ankle. Beyond that was an artificial leg, made of wood and plastic!